SEARCH IN A DARK COUNTRY . . .

A bookkeeper named Fredrich Schirmer had died at Bad Schwennheim in 1939. He had a son named Johann. Find this son. If he was dead, then find his heir.

Those were George's instructions.

There were probably thousands of Johann Schirmers in Germany, but certain things were known about this one.

And certain things were not.

It was these things that were mysterious. And treacherous. And very possibly, deadly.

THE SCHIRMER INHERITANCE

Other thrillers by Eric Ambler
published by Ballantine Books:

THE

Schirmer
Inheritance

Eric Ambler

BALLANTINE BOOKS • NEW YORK

ISBN 0-345-25916-5

This edition published by arrangement with Alfred A. Knopf, Inc.

Manufactured in the United States of America

First Ballantine Books Edition: August 1977

To
SYLVIA PAYNE

Prologue

IN 1806 Napoleon set out to chastise the King of Prussia. Both at Auerstadt and at Jena the Prussian armies suffered crushing defeats. Then, what remained of them marched east to join a Russian army under Bennigsen. In the following February, Napoleon met this combined force at the town of Preussisch-Eylau, near Königsberg.

Eylau was one of the bloodiest and most terrible of Napoleon's battles. It began in a blizzard and in a temperature well below freezing-point. Both armies were half starved and fought with desperate ferocity for the bleak shelter of the buildings of Eylau itself. Casualties on both sides were heavy, nearly a quarter of those engaged being killed. When, at nightfall on the second day, the fighting ended, it was from exhaustion rather than because a decision had been reached. Then, during the night, the Russian army began to retreat northward. The survivors of the Prussian corps, whose flank-guard action against Ney's troops had nearly served to win the day, now had no reason to remain. They made their withdrawal through the village of Kuttschitten to the east. The cavalry screen of their rear guard was provided by the Dragoons of Ansbach.

The relationship between this unit and the rest of the Prussian army was absurd, but in the middle Europe of the period, not unusually so. Not many years before, and well within the memories of the older soldiers in it, the regiment had been the only mounted force in the independent principality of Ansbach, and had taken its oaths of allegiance to the ruling Margrave. Then, Ansbach had fallen upon evil times and the last Mar-

1

grave had sold his land and his people to the King of Prussia. Fresh oaths of allegiance had had to be sworn. Yet their new lord had eventually proved as fickle as the old. In the year before Eylau the Dragoons had experienced a further change of status. The province of Ansbach had been ceded by the Prussians to Bavaria. As Bavaria was an ally of Napoleon, this meant that, strictly speaking, the Ansbachers should now have been fighting against the Prussians, not beside them. However, the Dragoons themselves were as indifferent to the anomaly they constituted as they were to the cause for which they fought. The conception of nationality meant little to them. They were professional soldiers in the eighteenth-century meaning of the term. If they had marched and fought and suffered and died for two days and a night, it was neither for love of the Prussians nor from hatred of Napoleon; it was because they had been trained to do so, because they hoped for the spoils of victory, and because they feared the consequences of disobedience.

Thus, as his horse picked its way through the woods on the outskirts of Kuttschitten that night, Sergeant Franz Schirmer was able to consider his situation and make plans for extricating himself from it, without much inconvenience to his conscience. Not many of the Dragoons of Ansbach were left, and of those who were, few would survive the hardships to come. The wounded and the badly frostbitten would die first, and then, when the horses had been lost or eaten, starvation and sickness would kill off all but the youngest and strongest of the remainder. Twenty-four hours earlier the Sergeant could reasonably have expected to be one of the enduring few. Now he could not. Late that afternoon he had himself been wounded.

The wound had affected him strangely. A French cuirassier had slashed with a sabre, and the Sergeant had taken the blow on his right arm. The blade had sliced obliquely through the heavy deltoid muscles and down to the bone just above the elbow. It was an ugly wound, but the bone had not broken and it had therefore been unnecessary for him to seek torture at

2

the hands of the army surgeons. A comrade had bound up the wound for him and strapped the arm against his chest with a crossbelt. It throbbed painfully now, but the bleeding seemed to have stopped. He was very weak, but that, he thought, might be due to hunger and the cold rather than to any serious loss of blood. The thing he found so strange was that with all his physical distress there went an extraordinary feeling of well-being.

It had come upon him as the wound was being bandaged. The feelings of surprise and terror with which he had first regarded the blood pouring down his useless arm had suddenly gone, and in their place had been an absurd, splendid sense of freedom and light-heartedness.

He was a bovine young man of a practical turn of mind, not given to fancies. He knew something about wounds. His had been bound up in its own blood and could therefore be reckoned healthy; but there was still no more than an even chance of his escaping death from gangrene. He knew something about war, too, and could see not only that the battle was probably lost but also that retreat would take them into a countryside already picked clean by armies on the move. Yet this knowledge brought no despair with it. It was as if he had received with his wound some special forgiveness for his sins, an absolution more potent and complete than that which any mortal priest could give. He felt that he had been touched by God Himself, and that any drastic steps he might be obliged to take in order to stay alive would have Divine approval.

His horse stumbled as it fought its way clear a snowdrift, and the Sergeant reined in. Half the officers had been killed and he had been put in command of one of the outlying detachments. He had orders to keep well out on the flank away from the road, and for a while it had been easy to do so; but now they had emerged from the forest, and in the deep snow the going was bad. One or two of the Dragoons behind him had already dismounted and were leading their horses. He could hear them floundering about in the snow at the rear of the column. If it proved necessary for him to lead his own horse he might not have the strength to get back into the saddle.

He thought about this for a moment. After a two-day battle fought so desperately, the chances of there being any French cavalry still capable of harrying the retreat from a flank were remote. The flank guard was therefore no more than a drillbook precaution. Certainly it was not worth taking risks for. He gave a brief word of command and the column began to turn into the forest again towards the road. He had no great fear of his disobedience being discovered. If it were, he would simply say that he had lost his way; he would not be severely punished for failing to do an officer's duty. In any case, he had more important matters to consider.

Food was the first thing.

Luckily, the haversack beneath his long cloak still contained most of the frozen potatoes he had looted from a farm building the previous day. They must be eaten sparingly; and secretly. At times like these, a man known to have private stores of food went in some danger, whatever his rank. However, the potatoes would not last long and there would be no soup pots bubbling at the end of this march. Even the horses would be better off. None of the supply wagons had been lost and there was a day's fodder still in them. The men would starve first.

He fought down a rising sense of panic. He would have to do something soon and panic would not help him. Already he could feel the cold eating into him. Not many hours could elapse before fever and exhaustion took irrevocable charge of the situation. His knees tightened involuntarily on the saddle flaps, and at that moment the idea came to him.

The horse had started and passaged a little at the pressure. Sergeant Schirmer relaxed his thigh muscles and, leaning forward, patted the animal's neck affectionately with his left hand. He was smiling to himself

4

as the horse walked on again. By the time the detachment reached the road his plan was made.

For the rest of that night and most of the next day the Prussian corps moved slowly eastward towards the Masurian Lakes; then it turned north to Insterburg. Soon after nightfall, and on the pretext of rounding up a straggler, Sergeant Schirmer left the detachment and rode south across the frozen lakes in the general direction of Lötzen. By morning he was south of that town.

He was also nearly at the limit of his strength. The march from Eylau to the point at which he had deserted had been bad enough; the cross-country journey from there would have taxed even an unwounded man. Now, the pain of his arm was at moments intolerable and he was shaking so much from fever and the bitter cold that he could scarcely stay in the saddle. He was beginning to wonder, indeed, if he might not have been mistaken in his estimate of God's intentions, and if what he had supposed to be a sign of Divine favour might not prove to have been an intimation of approaching death. He knew, at all events, that if he did not very soon find shelter of the kind his plan called for, he would die.

He reined in and with an effort raised his head again to look about him. Far away to the left across the white desolation of a frozen lake he could see the low black shape of a farmhouse. His eyes moved on. It was just possible that there was a nearer building to investigate. But there was nothing. Hopelessly he turned his horse's head in the direction of the farmhouse and resumed his march.

The area into which the Sergeant had ridden was, although at that date part of the Kingdom of Prussia, inhabited mainly by Poles. It had never been very prosperous; and after the Russian army had passed through it, commandeering the winter stores of grain and fodder and herding away the livestock, it was little more than a wasteland. In some villages the Cossack horses had eaten the very thatch from the roofs, and in others the houses had been gutted by fire. The

5

campaigns of the armies of Holy Russia could be more devastating for her allies than for her enemies.

The Sergeant, himself an experienced campaigner, had not been unprepared for devastation. Indeed, his plan had depended upon it. Country that had just supplied a Russian army would not attract another army for some time to come. A deserter might consider himself reasonably safe there. What he had not been prepared for, however, was the absence of a starving population. Since dawn he had passed several farmhouses, and every one had been abandoned. He had realized by now that the Russians had been more exacting even than usual (perhaps because they had been dealing with Poles), and that the inhabitants, unable to conceal enough food to keep them alive until the spring, had trekked to places farther south that might have been spared. For him, therefore, the situation was desperate. He could perhaps stay in the saddle for another hour. If all the peasants in the immediate vicinity had gone with the rest he was finished. He raised his head again, blinking to free his eyelashes from the ice that clung to them, and peered ahead.

At that moment he saw the smoke.

It came in a thin wisp from the roof of the building he was heading for, and he saw it for only a moment before it disappeared. He was still some way off, but he was in no doubt as to what he had seen. This was a peat-burning area and that was smoke from a peat fire. His spirits rose as he urged his horse forward.

It took him another half-hour to reach the farmhouse. As he approached he saw that it was a wretched and dilapidated place. There was a low wooden building which was both barn and living-quarters, an empty sheep-pen, and a broken-down wagon almost hidden under a drift of snow. That was all.

The horse's hoofs made only a faint crunching sound in the frozen snow. As he drew nearer, he let go the reins and carefully eased his carbine from its long saddle-holster. When he had primed it he wedged the weapon across the saddlebags and against the rolled blankets at the pommel. Then he took up the reins again and went on.

At one end of the building there was a small shuttered window, and beside it a door. The snow outside had been trodden since the last fall, but except for the slight trickle of peat smoke from the roof, there was no other sign of life. He stopped and looked about him. The gate of the sheep-pen was open. Near the cart was a slight mound of snow that probably covered the remains of a hayrick. There were no cattle droppings on the fresh snow, no sounds of poultry. But for the faint sighing of the wind, the silence was absolute. The Russians had taken everything.

He let the reins slip through his fingers, and the horse shook its head. The jangling of the bit seemed very loud. He looked quickly at the door of the building. If the sound had been heard, the first response to it would be that of fear; and, providing that it led to the immediate opening of the door and prompt compliance with his wishes, fear would be useful. If it led to the door's being barricaded against him, however, he was in a difficulty. He would have to break the door down, and he could not risk dismounting until he was sure that this was to be the end of his journey.

He waited. There was no sound from within. The door remained shut. His Dragoon's instinct was to slam the butt of his carbine against it and yell at those inside to come out or be killed; but he put the temptation aside. The carbine butt might have to come into play later, but for the present he would try the friendly approach he had planned.

He tried to call "Ho!" but the sound that came from his throat was no more than a sob. Disconcerted, he tried again.

"Ho!"

He managed to croak the word this time, but a deadly feeling of helplessness swept over him. He, who a moment ago had been thinking of battering on a door with his carbine and even of breaking it down, had not enough strength left to shout. There was a roaring in his ears and he thought he was going to fall. He shut

7

his eyes, fighting down the horrible sensation. As he opened his eyes again, he saw the door slowly open.

The face of the woman who stood in the doorway looking up at him was so ravaged by hunger that it was hard to tell what her age might be. But for the braids of hair wound round her head, even her sex would have been in doubt. The voluminous peasant rags she wore were quite shapeless and her feet and legs were bound with sacking like a man's. She stared at him dully, then said something in Polish and turned to go inside. He leaned forward and spoke in German.

"I am a Prussian soldier. There has been a great battle. The Russians are defeated."

He said it as if he were announcing a victory. She stopped and looked up again. Her sunken eyes were quite expressionless. He had the curious idea that they would remain so even if he were to draw his sabre and cut her down.

"Who else is here?" he said.

Her lips moved again and this time she spoke in German. "My father. He was too weak to go with our neighbours. What do you want here?"

"What's the matter with him?"

"He has the wasting fever."

"Ah!" If it had been the plague, he would have chosen to die in the snow rather than stay.

"What do you want?" she repeated.

To answer her, he undid the fastenings of his cloak and threw it back to reveal his wounded arm.

"I need shelter and rest," he said; "and someone to cook my food until my wound is healed."

Her eyes flickered from his bloodstained tunic to the carbine and the bulging saddlebags beneath it. He guessed that she was thinking that if she had the strength she might seize the gun and kill him. He put his hand on it firmly and her eyes met his again.

"There is no food to cook," she said.

"I have plenty of food," he answered; "enough to share with those who help me."

She still stared at him. He nodded reassuringly; then, holding his carbine firmly in his left hand, he brought

8

his right leg across the saddle and slid to the ground. As his feet touched it, his legs gave way under him and he sprawled in the snow. A burning shaft of agony shot from his arm through every nerve in his body. He screamed, and then, for a moment of two after, lay there sobbing. At last, still clutching the carbine, he clambered dizzily to his feet.

The woman had made no attempt to help him. She had not even moved. He pushed past her through the doorway into the hovel beyond.

Inside, he looked round warily. By the light from the doorway that filtered through the peat smoke he could dimly see a rough wooden bed with what looked like a pile of sacking on it. A whimpering sound came from it now. The peat fire glowed dully in a crude clay stove in the centre. The dirt floor was soft with ash and peat dust. The reeking air made him choke. He blundered round the stove and between the roof supports into the space where the animals had been kept. The straw under his feet here was filthy but he kicked a pile of it together against the back of the stove. He knew that the woman had followed him in and gone over to the sick man. Now he heard a whispered conversation. He arranged the pile of straw into the semblance of a bed and when he had finished spread his cloak on it. The whispers had ceased. He heard a movement behind him and turned.

The woman stood there facing him. She had a small axe in her hands.

"The food," she said.

He nodded and went out into the yard again. She followed and stood watching as, with his carbine held between his knees, he awkwardly unstrapped the blankets. He succeeded at last and flung the roll in the snow.

"The food," she said again.

He raised the carbine and, pressing the butt against his left hip, slid his hand down to the lock. With an effort he managed to cock it and move his forefinger on to the trigger. Then he put the muzzle to the horse's head just below the ear.

"Here is our food," he said, and pulled the trigger.

His ears sang with the noise of the shot as the horse sank kicking to the ground. The carbine had leaped from his hand and lay in the snow, smoking. He picked up the blankets and tucked them under his arm before retrieving it. The woman still stood watching him. He nodded to her and, motioning to the horse, went towards the house.

Almost before he reached the door, she was on her knees by the dying animal, at work on it with the axe. He looked back. There was the saddle and its contents; his sabre too. She might easily kill him with it while he lay helpless. There was a fortune, by her standards, in the flat leather pouch beneath his tunic. For a moment he watched the quick, desperate movements of her arms and the dark mess of blood spreading in the snow beneath her. His sabre? She would not need a sabre if she had a mind to kill him.

Then he felt the periodic agony of his arm returning and heard himself beginning to moan. He knew suddenly that there was nothing more he could do now to order the world outside his own body. He stumbled through the doorway and to his bed. The carbine he put on the ground under the cloak. Then he took off his helmet, unrolled his blankets, and lay down in the warm darkness to fight for his life.

The woman's name was Maria Dutka, and she was eighteen when Sergeant Schirmer first set eyes on her. Her mother had died when she was young and, as there were no other children and her father had failed to find a second wife, Maria had been brought up to do the work of a son and heir on the holding. Moreover, the chronic disease from which Dutka suffered was now of long standing and the periods of relief from it had become rarer. She was already accustomed to thinking and acting for herself.

She was not headstrong, however. Although the idea of killing the Sergeant, in order to avoid having to share the dead horse with him, did occur to her, she discussed the matter with her father first. She was by nature deeply superstitious, and when he suggested that

10

some supernatural agency might have had a hand in the Sergeant's providential appearance, she saw the danger of her plan. She saw, too, that even if the Sergeant were to die of his wound—and he was very near to death in those first days—the supernatural powers might consider that her murderous thoughts about him had turned the scale.

She nursed him, accordingly, with a kind of anxious devotion which it was easy for the grateful Sergeant to misunderstand. Later, however, she did something that appealed to him still more. When, during his convalescence, he made an attempt to thank her for so faithfully keeping her part of their bargain, she explained her motives to him with great simplicity and candour. At the time he was both amused and impressed. Afterwards, when he thought about what she had said and the fact that she had said it, he experienced rather more surprising sensations. As the food they shared restored her youthful appearance and vitality, he began to watch the movements of her body and to modify pleasurably his earlier plans for the future.

He stayed in the Dutka house for eight months. Preserved under the snow, the carcass of the horse supplied them all with fresh meat until the thaw came, and then with the smoked and dried remains. By that time, too, the Sergeant was able to take his carbine into the woods and bring back deer. Vegetables began to grow. Then, for a few remarkable weeks, old Dutka rallied and, with the Sergeant and Maria doing a horse's work in the traces, was even able in the end to plough his land.

The Sergeant's continued presence was taken as a matter of course now. Neither Maria nor her father ever referred to his military past. He was a victim of war, as they were. The returning neighbours found nothing strange in his presence. They themselves had spent the winter working for strangers. If old Dutka had found a strong, hard-working Prussian to help him set things to rights, so much the better. And should the curious wonder how old Dutka paid him or why

11

a Prussian should trouble to work so poor a patch of land, there was always someone to remind them of Maria's broad hips and strong legs and of the harvest to be reaped between them by such a lusty young fellow.

The summer came. The battle of Friedland was fought. The Emperors of France and Russia met on a raft moored in the river Niemen. The Treaty of Tilsit was signed. Prussia was stripped of all her territories west of the Elbe and all her Polish provinces. Bialla, only a few miles south of the Dutkas' holding, was suddenly on the Russian frontier, and Lyck had become a garrison town. Prussian infantry patrols came seeking recruits, and the Sergeant took to the woods with the other young men. He was away on one of these excursions when Maria's father died.

After the burial ceremonies he got out his leather money-pouch and sat down with Maria to count his savings. The proceeds of many looting forays and the peculations of four years as a non-commissioned officer, they were more than sufficient to match the small amount that Maria would get from the sale of her father's holding to a neighbour. For there was no question now of their remaining to work the land. They had seen what could happen when the Russian armies came, and with this new frontier the Russians were no more than a day's march away. To them this seemed a weightier argument for leaving the holding than the Sergeant's precarious position as a deserter. The place for them to go was clearly somewhere where there were neither Russians nor Prussians, and where Maria, already pregnant, could bring up their children in the certainty of being able to feed them.

Early in the November of 1807 they set out, with a handcart contrived from Dutka's old wagon, to walk towards the west. It was a hard, dangerous journey, for their road lay through Prussia and they dared travel only at night. But they did not go hungry. They had brought their food with them in the cart and it lasted until they reached Wittenberg. That was the first town they entered in broad daylight, too. They were free of Prussian soil at last.

They did not remain in Wittenberg, however. To the Sergeant it seemed uncomfortably near the Prussian border. Towards the middle of December they arrived in Mühlhausen, newly incorporated into the Kingdom of Westphalia. There, Maria's first son, Karl, was born; and there, Maria and the Sergeant were married. For a time, the Sergeant worked as an ostler; but later, when he had added to their savings, he set up in business as a horse-coper.

He prospered. The tides of the Napoleonic wars washed gently in the harbour that he and Maria had found. For several years it seemed as though the evil days were over. Then, the disease from which her father had suffered attacked Maria herself. Two years after the birth of her second son, Hans, she died.

Eventually Sergeant Schirmer married again and had ten more children by his second wife. He died in 1850, a respected and successful man.

Only once during all those happy years in Mühlhausen was Franz Schirmer disturbed by memories of the military crime he had committed. In 1815, by the Treaty of Paris, Mühlhausen became a Prussian city.

It was the year of the Sergeant's second marriage, and while he did not think it likely that church records would be combed for the names of deserters, there was always a chance that they might be used in checking mobilization lists. He could not bring himself to be fatalistic about the risk. After so many years' immunity from arrest he had lost the habit of living for the moment. The prospect of death before a firing-squad, however remote it might be, could never be endured with the old fortitude.

Then what was to be done? He gave the matter careful thought. In the past, he reminded himself, he had trusted in God; and in times of great danger God had been good to him. But could he *still* simply trust in God? And was this, he asked himself critically, a time of *great* danger? After all, there were plenty of other Schirmers in the Prussian army records; and

13

some of them, no doubt, were men named Franz. Was it really necessary to call upon God to insure against the possibility of the list of those citizens who had purchased army exemptions in Mühlhausen being compared with the list of army deserters in Potsdam? Or really wise to do so? Might not God, who had done so much for His servant, be displeased at having this minor responsibility thrust upon Him and so neglect it? Was there not, therefore, something that His servant could do for himself in the matter, without invoking the aid of the Almighty?

Yes indeed, there was!

He decided to change his name to Schneider.

He encountered only one slight difficulty. It was simple to change his own surname and that of the baby, Hans. He had good friends in the mayor's office, and his excuse that there was another horse-dealer of the same name in a near-by town was readily accepted. But the first son, Karl, presented a problem. The boy, now seven years old, had just been classified for future conscription by the Prussian military authorities, and the Sergeant neither had nor wanted friends in Prussian military circles. Moreover, any official move to change the boy's name might easily invite the very inquiries into origins which he most dreaded. In the end he did nothing about Karl's name. So it was that, although the sons of Franz and Maria were baptized in the name of Schirmer, they grew up with different surnames. Karl remained Karl Schirmer; Hans became Hans Schneider.

The Sergeant's change of name never caused him a moment's anxiety or inconvenience in his lifetime. The anxiety and inconvenience resulting from it descended, over a hundred years later, on the head of Mr. George L. Carey.

1

GEORGE CAREY came from a Delaware family that looked like an illustration for an advertisement of an expensive make of car. His father was a prosperous doctor with snow-white hair. His mother came from an old Philadelphia family and was an important member of the garden club. His brothers were tall, solid, and handsome. His sisters were slim, strong, and vivacious. All had fine regular teeth, which showed when they smiled. The whole family, indeed, looked so happy, so secure, and so successful that it was difficult not to suspect that the truth about them might be different. But no, they actually were happy, secure, and successful. They were also exceedingly smug.

George was the youngest son and, although his shoulders were not so broad as those of his brothers nor his smile as self-satisfied, he was the most talented and intelligent member of the family. When the glories of their football-playing days had departed, his brothers had made their ways aimlessly into business. George's plans for the future had been clear-cut from the moment he left high school. Despite his father's hope for a successor in his practice, George had declined to pretend to an interest in medicine which he did not feel. What he wanted to go in for was law; and not the criminal, courtroom kind, but the kind that led in early middle age to the presidencies of railroads and steel corporations or to high political office. But while the war, which came just after he had been graduated from Princeton, had removed much of his solemnity and smugness and had had beneficial effects upon his sense of humour, it had done nothing to change his mind about his chosen profession. After four and a half years as a bomber pilot, he went to Harvard Law School. He graduated, *cum laude*, early in 1949. Then, having spent a useful year as secretary to a learned and famous judge, he joined Lavater, Powell and Sistrom.

The firm of Lavater, Powell and Sistrom of Philadelphia is one of the really important law offices of the eastern United States, and the long list of partners reads like a selection of promising candidates for a vacancy on the Supreme Court. No doubt its massive reputation still derives to some extent from memories of the vast utilities manipulations with which it was concerned in the twenties; but there have been few corporation cases of any magnitude during the last thirty years in which the firm has not held an important brief. It remains a virile, forward-looking concern, and to be invited to join it is a mark of approbation most flattering to a young lawyer.

Thus, as he arranged his belongings in one of Lavater's comfortably furnished offices, George had reason to feel satisfied with the progress of his career. Admittedly, he was a little old for the somewhat junior position he occupied, but he was shrewd enough to realize that his four years in the Air Corps had not been wholly wasted from a professional point of view, and that the distinction of his war record had had quite as much to do with his presence at the Lavater firm as his work at law school or the warm recommendations of the learned judge. Now, if all went well (and why shouldn't it?), he could look forward to rapid advancement, valuable contacts, and an expanding personal reputation. He felt that he had arrived.

The news that he was to do some work on the Schneider Johnson case came, then, as a disagreeable blow. It was also a surprise of another kind. The sort of business that Lavater, Powell and Sistrom normally handled was the sort that made reputations as surely as it made money. From what George remembered of the Schneider Johnson case, it was just the sort of

16

slapstick affair that a corporation lawyer with a thought for his reputation would pay to stay clear of.

It had been one of the notorious missing-heir-to-a-fortune absurdities of the pre-war years.

In 1938, Amelia Schneider Johnson, a senile old woman of eighty-one, had died in Lamport, Pennsylvania. She had lived alone in the decrepit frame house which had been the late Mr. Johnson's wedding present to her, and her declining years had been passed in an atmosphere of genteel poverty. When she had died, however, it had been found that her estate included three million dollars in bonds which she had inherited in the twenties from her brother, Martin Schneider, a soft-drink tycoon. She had had an eccentric distrust of banks and safe-deposit boxes and had kept the bonds in a tin trunk under her bed. She had also distrusted lawyers and had made no will. In Pennsylvania, at the time, the law governing intestacy had been determined by an act of 1917 which said, in effect, that anyone with even a remote blood-relationship to the deceased might be entitled to a share in the estate. Amelia Schneider Johnson's only known relative had been an elderly spinster, Miss Clothilde Johnson; but she had been a sister-in-law and therefore had not qualified under the act. With the enthusiastic and disastrous co-operation of the newspapers, a search for Amelia's blood-relations had begun.

It was, George thought, all too easy to understand the newspapers' eagerness. They had scented another Garrett case. Old Mrs. Garrett had died in 1930, leaving seventeen million dollars and no will, and here was the case eight years later, still going strong, with three thousand lawyers still chiselling away, twenty-six thousand claimants to the money, and a fine smell of corruption over all. The Schneider Johnson thing could last as long. True, it was smaller, but size wasn't everything. It had plenty of human angles—a fortune at stake, the romantic isolation of the old lady's declining years (she had lost her only son in the Argonne), the lonely death without a relative at the bedside, the fruitless search for the will—there was no reason why

17

it should not have staying-power, too. The name Schneider and its American modifications were widely distributed. The old girl must have had blood-relatives somewhere even if she hadn't known them. Or him! Or her! Yes, there might even turn out to be a one hundred per cent non-sharing heir! All right, then, where was he? Or she? On a farm in Wisconsin? In a real-estate office in California? Behind the counter of a drugstore in Texas? Which of the thousands of Schneiders, Snyders, and Sniders in America was going to be the lucky one? Who was the unsuspecting millionaire? Corn? Well, maybe, but always good for a follow-up, and of nation-wide interest.

And of nation-wide interest it had proved. By the beginning of 1939, the administrator of the estate had been notified of over eight thousand claims to be the missing heir, an army of disreputable lawyers had moved in to exploit the claimants, and the whole case had begun to soar rapidly into the cloud-cuckoo land of high fantasy, skullduggery, and court-room farce in which it was to remain until, on the outbreak of war, it had fallen suddenly into oblivion.

What business Lavater, Powell and Sistrom could have with the resurrection of so unsavoury a corpse, George could not imagine.

It was Mr. Budd, one of the senior partners, who enlightened him.

The main burden of the Schneider Johnson estate had been borne by Messrs. Moreton, Greener and Cleek, an old-fashioned Philadelphia law firm of great respectability. They had been Miss Clothilde Johnson's attorneys and had conducted the formal search for a will on her instructions. The intestacy duly established, the matter had come before the Orphans' Court in Philadelphia, and the Register of Wills had appointed Robert L. Moreton as administrator of the estate. He had remained the administrator until the end of 1944.

"And very nice too," said Mr. Budd. "If only he'd had the sense to leave it at that, I wouldn't have blamed him. But no, the cockle-brained old coot retained his *own* firm as attorneys for the administrator. Jeepers, in a case like that it was suicidal!"

Mr. Budd was a pigeon-chested man with a long head, a neat, clipped moustache, and bifocal glasses. He had a ready smile, a habit of using out-of-date colloquialisms, and an air of careless good-humour of which George was deeply suspicious.

"The combined fees," George said carefully, "must have been pretty big on an estate of that size."

"No fees," declared Mr. Budd, "are big enough to make it worth while for a decent law office to get mixed up with a lot of ambulance-chasers and crooks. There are dozens of these inheritance cases hanging fire all over the world. Look at the Abdul Hamid estate! The British got tied up in that one and it's been going on for thirty years or more. That'll probably never be settled. Look at the Garrett case! Think how many reputations that's damaged. Shucks! It's always the same. Is A an imposter? Is B out of his mind? Who died before whom? Is the old photograph Aunt Sarah or Aunt Flossie? Has a forger been at work with faded ink?" He waved his arms disparagingly. "I tell you, George, in my opinion the Schneider Johnson case pretty well finished Moreton, Greener and Cleek as a regular law firm. And when Bob Moreton got sick in '44 and had to retire, that was the end. They dissolved."

"Couldn't Greener or Cleek have taken over as administrator?"

Mr. Budd pretended to look shocked. "My dear George, you don't take over an appointment like that. It's a reward for good and faithful service. In this case, our learned, highly respected, and revered John J. Sistrom was the lucky man."

"Oh. I see."

"The investments do the work, George, our John J. takes the fees as administrator. However," Mr. Budd continued with a trace of satisfaction in his voice, "it doesn't look as if he's going to do so much longer. You'll see why in a moment. From what old Bob Moreton told me at the time, the position was originally this. Amelia's father was named Hans Schneider. He was a German who'd immigrated in 1849. Bob Moreton and his partners were pretty well convinced in the end that, if there were anybody at all entitled to take the estate, it was one of the old man's relatives back in Germany. But the whole thing was complicated by the representation question. Do you know anything about that, George?"

"Bregy, discussing the 1947 act, gives a very clear summary of the former rules."

"That's dandy." Mr. Budd grinned. "Because, frankly, I don't know a thing about it. Now, leaving out all the newspaper nonsense, here's what happened to the case. In '39 old Bob Moreton went off to Germany to check up on the other side of the Schneider family. Self-preservation, of course. He needed facts to go on if he was going to deal with all those phony claims. Then, when he got back, the damnedest thing happened. The damnedest things were always happening on that screwy case. It seemed that the Nazis had got wind of Bob's inquiries. What they did was to take a quick look into the thing themselves and produce an old man named Rudolph Schneider. Then they claimed the whole estate on his behalf."

"I remember that," George said. "They hired McClure to act for them."

"That's right. This Rudolph was from Dresden or some such place and they said that he was a first cousin of Amelia Johnson. Moreton, Greener and Cleek fought the claim. Said the documents the Krauts produced were forged. Anyway, the case was still before the courts when we got into the war in '41, and that finished it as far as they were concerned. The Alien Property Custodian in Washington moved in and filed a claim. Because of the German claim of course. The case froze. When he retired, Bob Moreton handed over all the documents to John J. There were over two tons of them and they're down in our vaults right now, just where they were left when Moreton, Greener and Cleek delivered them in '44. Nobody's ever troubled

20

to look them over. No reason to. Well, now there *is* a reason."

George's heart sank. "Oh, yes?"

By choosing this moment to fill his pipe Mr. Budd avoided George's eyes as he went on. "This is the situation, George. It seems that with the appreciation of values and interest the estate is worth over four million now and the Commonwealth of Pennsylvania has decided to exercise its rights under the act and claim the lot. However, they've asked John J., as administrator, if he proposes to fight them on it, and, just for form's sake, he feels we ought to check through the documents to make sure that there's no reasonable claim outstanding. So that's what I want you to do, George. Just check through for him. Make sure he's not overlooking anything. O.K.?"

"Yes, sir. O.K."

But he did not quite succeed in keeping a note of resignation out of his voice. Mr. Budd looked up with a sympathetic chuckle. "And if it'll make you feel any better about the job, George," he said, "I can tell you that we've been getting short of vault space for some time now. If you can get that load of junk out of the way you'll be earning the heartfelt thanks of the entire office."

George managed to smile.

2
═══

HE HAD no difficulty in finding the Schneider Johnson records. They were parcelled up in damp-proof wrappings and had a storage vault to themselves, which they filled from floor to ceiling. It was clear that Mr. Budd's estimate of their total weight had not been exaggerated.

Fortunately, all the parcels had been carefully labelled and arranged systematically. Having made sure that he understood the system which had been employed, George made a selection of the parcels and had them carried up to his office.

It was late in the afternoon when he started work and, with some idea of getting a general picture of the case before settling down to work seriously on the claims, he had brought up a bulky parcel labelled: "Schneider Johnson Press Clippings." The label proved to be slightly misleading. What in fact the parcel contained was the record of Messrs. Moreton, Greener and Cleek's hopeless battle with the press and their efforts to stem the flood of nonsensical claims that was overwhelming them. It made pathetic reading.

The record began two days after Mr. Moreton had been appointed administrator of the estate. A New York tabloid had discovered that Amelia's father, Hans Schneider ("the Old Forty-niner," as the paper called him), had married a New York girl named Mary Smith. This meant, the paper had contended excitedly, that the name of the missing heir could be Smith as well as Schneider.

Messrs. Moreton, Greener and Cleek, as attorneys for the administrator, had properly hastened to deny the contention; but instead of pointing out, more or less simply, that, as Amelia's first cousins on her mother's side had all been dead for years, the Smith family of New York did not qualify in law as heirs, they had stuffily contented themselves with quoting the act as saying that "there could be no representation admitted among collaterals after the grandchildren of brothers and sisters and children of aunts and uncles." This unfortunate sentence, quoted derisively under the subheading "Double-Talk," was the only part of the statement that had been printed.

Most of the partners' subsequent statements had suffered the same kind of fate. From time to time some of the more responsible papers had made serious efforts to interpret the intestacy laws to their readers, but never, as far as George could see, had the partners attempted to assist them. The fact that, as Amelia had had no close relatives living, the only possible heirs were any nephews and nieces of the late Hans Schneider who had still been alive when Amelia died, was never explicitly stated by the partners. The nearest they had come to clarity had been in a statement suggesting that it was unlikely that there were any "first cousins of the intestate decedent who had survived the decedent" in America, and that if any did exist they would most probably be found in Germany.

They might have saved themselves the trouble. The suggestion that the legal heir to the estate might be in Europe instead of somewhere like Wisconsin had not been interesting to the newspapers of 1939; the possibility of his not existing at all they had preferred to ignore altogether. Besides, the enterprise of a Milwaukee paper had just then given the story yet another twist. With the help of the immigration authorities, this paper's special investigator had been able to discover the number of families named Schneider who had emigrated from Germany in the latter half of the nineteenth century. The number was large. Was it too much to suppose, the paper had asked, that at least one of the Old Forty-niner's younger brothers had followed his example in emigrating? No indeed! The hunt had been on again, and squads of special investigators had gone forth to pad hopefully through city records, land registers, and state archives in the footsteps of the immigrant Schneiders.

George repacked the parcel with a sigh. He knew already that he was not going to enjoy the next few weeks.

The total number of claims made was just over eight thousand and he found that there was a separate file for each. Most had only two or three letters in them, but many were quite thick, while some had parcels to themselves and bulged with affidavits, photostats of documents, tattered photographs, and genealogical tables. A few had old Bibles and other family souvenirs in them, and one, for some inexplicable reason, even contained a greasy fur cap.

George set to work. By the end of his first week he had been through seven hundred of the claims and was feeling sorry for Messrs. Moreton, Greener and Cleek. Many, of course, had come from lunatics and cranks. There was the angry man in North Dakota who said that *his* name was Martin Schneider, that he was *not* dead, and that Amelia Johnson had stolen the money from him while he lay sleeping. There was the woman who claimed the estate on behalf of a California society for the propagation of the Cataphrygian heresy, on the grounds that the spirit of the late Amelia had entered into Mrs. Schultz, the society's honorary treasurer. And there was the man, writing in multi-coloured inks from a state hospital, who said that he was the legitimate son of Amelia by a secret first marriage to a coloured man. But the majority of the claimants seemed to be persons who, while not actually insane, had rudimentary notions of what constituted evidence. There was, for instance, a Chicago man named Higgins who had evolved an elaborate claim from the memory of having heard his father say that Cousin Amelia was a wicked old miser; and another man had pressed for a share of the estate on the strength of an old letter from a Danish relative named Schneider. Then there were those who warily declined to send evidence to support their claims lest it should be stolen and used to prove the case of another claimant, and others who demanded travelling expenses in order that they might present their cases in person to the administrator. Above all, there were the lawyers.

Only thirty-four out of the first seven hundred claims which George examined had been handled by attorneys, but it took him over two days to get through those particular files. The claims in question were mostly of doubtful validity, and one or two were patently dishonest. In George's view, no reputable lawyer would have touched any of them. But these had been disreputable lawyers; they had both touched and held on. They had quoted non-existent precedents and photographed useless documents. They had hired dishonest inquiry agents to conduct pointless investigations, and

24

quack genealogists to draw up faked family trees. They had written portentous letters and uttered obscure threats. The only thing, apparently, that none of them had ever done was to advise his client to withdraw a claim. In one of these files there was a letter to the administrator from an old woman named Snyder, regretting that she had no more money left to pay her attorney to act for her, and asking that her claim should not on this account be overlooked.

In his second week on the records, George managed, in spite of a severe cold in the head, to push his score of examined claims up to nineteen hundred. In the third week he topped three thousand. By the end of the fourth week he was at the halfway mark. He was also feeling very depressed. The boring nature of the work and the cumulative effect of so much evidence of human stupidity were lowering in themselves. The amused commiseration of his new colleagues and the knowledge that he was beginning his career in Lavater, Powell and Sistrom at the wrong end of an office joke had done nothing to improve matters. Mr. Budd, when last encountered in the elevator on his way back from lunch, had talked cheerfully about baseball and had not even troubled to ask for a progress report. On the Monday morning of the fifth week George surveyed with loathing the stacks of records that still remained to be examined.

"Finish the O's, Mr. Carey?" The speaker was the janitor who looked after the vaults, cleaned up the parcels, and carried them to and from George's office.

"No, I'd better start on the P's now."

"I can ease the rest of the O's out if you like, Mr. Carey."

"All right, Charlie. If you can do it without bringing the lot down." The inroads he had already made on the towering stacks of parcels had gradually reduced the stability of the remainder.

"Sure, Mr. Carey," said Charlie. He took hold of a section near the floor and pulled. There was a slithering noise and a crash as an avalanche of parcels engulfed him. In the cloud of dust that followed the subsidence, he stumbled to his feet coughing and swearing, his hand held to his head. Blood began to pour from a long cut over his eye.

"For God's sake, Charlie, how did that happen?"

The janitor kicked something solid under the heap of parcels about him. "This damned thing caught me on the head, Mr. Carey," he explained. "Must have been stacked up in the middle somewhere."

"Do you feel all right?"

"Oh, sure. It's only a scratch. Sorry, Mr. Carey."

"You'd better get it fixed anyway."

When he had handed the janitor over to the care of one of the elevator men and the dust in the vault had settled again, George went in and examined the confusion. Both the O's and the P's had vanished under a rubble of S's and W's. He pushed several of the parcels aside and saw the reason for the janitor's cut eye. It was a large, black, japanned deed box of the kind that used to line the walls of old family lawyers. Stencilled on it in white paint were the words: "SCHNEIDER—CONFIDENTIAL."

George dragged the box clear of the parcels and tried to open it. It was locked and there was no key attached to either of the handles. He hesitated. His business in this case was with the claims files, and it was foolish to waste time satisfying his curiosity about the contents of an old deed box. On the other hand, it would take an hour to straighten out the mess at his feet. There was little point in his covering himself with dust and cobwebs in order to hasten the process, and Charlie would be back in a few minutes. He went into the janitor's room, took a cold chisel and a hammer from the tool rack, and returned to the box. A few blows cut through the thin metal around the tongue of the lock, and he was able to wrench the lid open.

At first sight, the contents seemed to be simply some personal belongings from Mr. Moreton's office. There was a calf-bound appointment book with his initials stamped on it in gold, an onyx desk set, a carved teak cigar box, a tool leather blotting pad, and a pair of leather-covered letter trays to match it. In one of the trays there was a hand towel, some aspirin tablets, and a bottle of vitamin capsules. George lifted the tray. Beneath it was a thick loose-leaf binder labelled: "GERMAN INQUIRY RE SCHNEIDER BY ROBERT L. MORETON, 1939." He glanced through a page or two, saw that it was in diary form, and put it aside for later reading. Underneath was a Manila folder containing a mass of photographs, mostly, it appeared, of German legal documents of some sort. The only other things in the box were a sealed package and a sealed envelope. On the package was written: "Correspondence between Hans Schneider and his wife, with other documents found by Hilton G. Greener and Robert L. Moreton among effects of late Amelia Schneider Johnson, Sept. 1938." On the envelope was written: "Photograph handed to R. L. M. by Father Weichs at Bad Schwennheim."

George put Mr. Moreton's personal things back in the deed box and took the rest of the contents up to his office. There the first thing he did was to open the sealed parcel.

The letters in it had been carefully numbered and initialled by Mr. Greener and Mr. Moreton. There were seventy-eight of them, all tied up in small packets with silk ribbon and with a pressed flower in each. George undid one of the packets. The letters in it belonged to the courtship period of Amelia's parents, Hans Schneider and Mary Smith. They showed that Hans had been working in a warehouse at the time and learning English, and that Mary had been learning German. George thought them formal, graceless, and dull. However, their value to Mr. Moreton must have been considerable, for they had probably made possible the speedy tracing of the Smith family concerned, and led to its elimination from the list of claimants.

George tied the packet up again and turned to an album of old photographs. In it there were photographs of Amelia and Martin as children, of their brother Frederick, who had died at the age of twelve, and, of course, of Hans and Mary. More interesting, because

27

it was even older, was a daguerreotype portrait of an old man with a vast beard.

He sat erect and very stern, his big hands grasping the arms of the photographer's chair, his head pressed hard against the back of it. The lips were full and determined. There was a heavy, strong face beneath the beard. The silvered copper plate on which the portrait had been made was glued to a red velvet mount. Beneath it Hans had written: *"Mein geliebt Vater, Franz Schneider. 1782-1850."*

The only other document was a thin, leather-bound notebook filled with Hans's spidery writing. It was written in English. On the first page, elaborately decorated with ornamental pen-strokes, was a description of the book's contents: "An Account of My Beloved Father's Heroic Part in the Battle of Preussisch-Eylau, fought in the year 1807, of His Wounding, and of His Meeting with My Beloved Mother, who Saved His Life. Set down by Hans Schneider for His Children in June 1867, that They may be Proud of the Name They Bear."

The Account began with the events leading up to Eylau and went on with descriptions of the various actions in which the Ansbach Dragoons had engaged the enemy, and of spectacular incidents in the battle: a Russian cavalry charge, the capture of a battery of guns, the decapitation of a French officer. Obviously, what Hans had written down was a legend learned at his father's knee. Parts of it still had the artless quality of a fairy tale; but as the account progressed, the middle-aged Hans could be seen perplexedly trying to reconcile his boyhood memories with his adult sense of reality. The writing of the Account, George thought, must have been a strange experience for him.

After his description of the battle, however, Hans's touch had become surer. The emotions of the wounded hero, his certainty that God was with him, his determination to do his duty until the end—these things were described with practised unction. And when the terrible moment of treachery came, when the cowardly Prussians had abandoned the wounded hero while he was helping a stricken comrade, Hans had let loose a torrent of Biblical denunciation. If God had not guided the hoofs of the hero's horse to the farmhouse of the gentle Maria Dutka, all would certainly have been over. As it was, Maria had been understandably suspicious of the Prussian uniform, and (as she had later confessed to the hero) her humane instincts had been all but overcome by her fears for her virtue and for her ailing father. In the end, of course, all had been well. When his wound was healed, the hero had brought his rescuer home in triumph. In the following year Hans's elder brother, Karl, had been born.

The Account concluded with a sanctimonious homily on the subjects of prayer-saying and the obtaining of forgiveness for sins. George skipped it and turned to Mr. Moreton's diary.

Mr. Moreton and an interpreter whom he had engaged in Paris had arrived in Germany towards the end of March 1939.

His plan had been simple; simple in intention, at all events. First he would retrace Hans Schneider's steps. Then, when he had found out where the Schneider family had lived, he would set about discovering what had happened to all Hans's brothers and sisters.

The first part of the plan had proved simple of execution. Hans had come from somewhere in Westphalia; and in 1849 a man of military age had had to have a permit to leave it. In Münster, the old state capital, Mr. Moreton had been able to find the record of Hans's departure. Hans had come from Mühlhausen and gone to Bremen.

In Bremen, a search in the port authority files of old ships' manifests had revealed that Hans Schneider of Mühlhausen had sailed in the *Abigail*, an English ship of six hundred tons, on May 10, 1849. This had checked with a reference, in one of Hans's letters to Mary Smith, to his voyage from Germany. Mr. Moreton had now concluded that he was tracing the right Hans Schneider. He had gone next to Mühlhausen.

Here, however, a baffling situation had awaited him. He had found that, although the church registers recorded marriages, baptisms, and burials as far back as the Thirty Years' War, none of them covering the years 1807 and 1808 contained any reference to the name of Schneider.

Mr. Moreton had brooded on this disappointment for twenty-four hours; then he had had an idea. He had gone back to the registers.

This time he had turned to those for 1850, the year of Franz Schneider's death. The facts of his death and burial had been recorded, and the location of the grave. Mr. Moreton had gone to inspect it. Now he had had a most disturbing surprise. A decaying memorial stone had supplied the confusing information that this was the resting place of Franz Schneider and his much beloved wife, Ruth. According to Hans's Account, his mother's name had been Maria.

Mr. Moreton had returned to the registers again. It had taken him a long time to work back from 1850 to 1815, but by the time he had done so, he had had the names of no less than ten of Franz Schneider's children and the date of his marriage to Ruth Vogel. He had also learned to his dismay that none of the children's names had been either Hans or Karl.

The idea that there must have been a previous marriage in some other city had soon occurred to him. But where could this earlier marriage have taken place? With what other towns had Franz Schneider been associated? From what town, for instance, had he been recruited into the Prussian army?

There had been only one place where that sort of question might be answered. Mr. Moreton and his interpreter had gone to Berlin.

It had taken Mr. Moreton until the end of March to cut through the swathes of Nazi red tape and dig far enough into the archives at Potsdam to get at the Napoleonic war diaries of the Ansbach Dragoons. It had taken him less than two hours to find out that between 1800 and 1850 the name of Schneider had figured only once in the nominal rolls of the regiment. A Wilhelm Schneider had been killed by a fall from his horse in 1803.

It had been a bitter blow. Mr. Moreton's entry in his diary for that day ended with the despondent words: "So I guess it's a wild-goose chase after all. Nevertheless I will make a check search tomorrow. If no result, will abandon inquiry as I consider inability to link Hans Schneider positively with Mühlhausen family in records makes further efforts pointless."

George turned the page and then stared blankly. The next entry in the diary consisted entirely of figures. They filled the page, line after line of them. The next page was the same, and the page after that. He flicked the pages over rapidly. With the exception of the date headings, every entry in the diary from then on—and it continued for over three months—was in figures. Moreover, the figures were in groups of five. Not only had Mr. Moreton decided after all *against* abandoning his inquiries in Germany, but he had thought it necessary to record the results of them in cipher.

George abandoned the diary and glanced through the file of photographed documents. He did not read German with great confidence even when it was printed in roman type. German handwriting of the traditional kind defeated him completely. These were all handwritten. Careful scrutiny of two or three of them revealed the fact that they referred to the births and deaths of people named Schneider, but this was scarcely surprising. He put them aside and opened the sealed envelope.

The photograph "handed to R. L. M. by Father Weichs at Bad Schwennheim" proved to be a dogeared, postcard-size portrait of a young man and a young woman sitting side by side on a professional photographer's rustic bench. The woman had a certain fluffy prettiness and was possibly pregnant. The man was nondescript. Their clothes were of the early 1920's. They looked like a prosperous working-class couple on their day off. There was a painted background of snow-covered pines behind them. Across the corner of it was written, in German script: *"Johann und Ilse."* The photographer's imprint on the mount showed that it had been taken in Zurich. There was nothing else in the envelope.

Charlie, the janitor, came in with a piece of adhesive plaster on his forehead and another load of parcels, and George got back to work on the claims. But that night he took the contents of the deed box back to his apartment and went through them carefully again.

He was in a difficulty. He had been asked to check on the claims to the estate received by the former administrator; nothing else. If the deed box had not fallen and cut the jaintor's head, he would probably not have noticed it. It would have been moved out of the way of the parcels of claims files and then left in the vault. He would have worked his way through the claims and then, no doubt, simply reported to Mr. Budd what Mr. Budd wanted to hear: that there were no outstanding claims worth discussing and that the Commonwealth of Pennsylvania could go ahead. Then he, George, would have been free of the whole wretched business and ready to be rewarded with an assignment more suited to his abilities. Now it looked as if he had a choice of two ways of making a fool of himself. One was by forgetting about the contents of the deed box and so running the risk of allowing Mr. Sistrom to make a serious blunder; the other was by plaguing Mr. Budd with idle fancies.

High political office and the presidencies of railroads seemed very far away that night. It was not until the early hours of the morning that he thought of a tactful way of putting the thing to Mr. Budd.

Mr. Budd received George's report with impatience.

"I don't even know if Bob Moreton's still alive," he said irritably. "In any case, all that this cipher stuff suggests to me is that the man was in an advanced stage of paranoia."

"Did he seem O.K. when you saw him in '44, sir?"

"He may have *seemed* O.K., but from what you show me it looks very much as if he wasn't."

"But he *did* go on with the inquiry, sir."

"What if he did?" Mr. Budd sighed. "Look, George, we don't want any complications in this business. We just want to get rid of the thing, and the sooner the better. I appreciate that you want to be thorough, but I should have thought it was very simple, really. You just get a German translator on these photographed documents, find out what they're all about, then check through the claims from people named Schneider and see if the documents refer in any way. That's straightforward enough, isn't it?"

George decided that the time for tactful handling had arrived. "Yes, sir. But what I had in mind was a way of speeding up the whole thing. You see, I haven't got through to the Schneider claims yet, but, judging by the volume of paper in the vault, there must be at least three thousand of them. Now, it's taken me nearly four weeks to check through that number of ordinary claims. The Schneider files are certain to take longer. But I've been looking into things and I have a hunch that if I can check with Mr. Moreton it may save a lot of time."

"Why? How do you mean?"

"Well, sir, I checked through some of the reports on that case he fought against the Rudolph Schneider claim and the German government. It seemed to me quite clear that Moreton, Greener and Cleek had a whole lot of facts at their disposal that the other side didn't have. I think they had very definite information that there was no Schneider heir alive."

Mr. Budd looked at him shrewdly. "Are you suggesting, George, that Moreton as administrator went on and established beyond doubt that there was no heir, and that he and his partners then kept quiet about the fact so that they could go on drawing fees from the estate?"

"It could be, sir, couldn't it?"

"Terrible minds some of you young men have!" Mr. Budd suddenly became jovial again. "All right, what's your point?"

"If we could have the results of Moreton's confidential inquiries, we might have enough information to make any further examination of all these claims unnecessary."

33

Mr. Budd stroked his chin. "I see. Yes, not bad, George." He nodded briskly. "O.K. If the old chap's alive and in his right mind, see what you can do. The quicker we can get out from under the whole thing, the better."

"Yes, sir," said George.

That afternoon he had a call from Mr. Budd's secretary to say that a check with Mr. Moreton's former club had disclosed that he was now living in retirement at Montclair, New Jersey. Mr. Budd had written to the old man asking him if he would see George.

Two days later a reply came from Mrs. Moreton. She said that her husband had been bedridden for some months, but that in view of former associations, and providing that Mr. Carey's visit was brief, Mr. Moreton would be glad to put his memory at Mr. Carey's disposal. Mr. Moreton slept afternoons. Perhaps Friday morning at eleven o'clock would be convenient to Mr. Carey.

"That must be his second wife," said Mr. Budd.

On the Friday morning, George put the deed box and all its original contents into the back of his car and drove out to Montclair.

3

THE HOUSE was a comfortable-looking place surrounded by several acres of well-kept garden, and it occurred to George that the financial fate of Messrs. Morton, Greener and Cleek had not been quite as disastrous as Mr. Budd had implied. The second Mrs. Moreton proved to be a lean woman in her late forties. She had a straight back, a brisk manner, and a patronizing smile. It seemed probable that she had been Mr. Moreton's nurse.

"Mr. Carey is it? You won't tire him, will you? He's allowed to sit up in the mornings at present, but we have to be careful. Coronary thrombosis." She led the way through to a glass-enclosed porch at the rear of the house.

Mr. Moreton was big and pink and flabby, like an athlete gone to seed. He had short white hair and very blue eyes, and there was still a trace of boyish good looks visible in the slack, puffy face. He was lying, propped up by cushions and swathed in a blanket, on a day-bed fitted with a book-rest. He greeted George eagerly, thrusting the book-rest aside and struggling into a sitting posture in order to shake hands. He had a soft, pleasant voice and smelled faintly of lavender water.

For a minute or two he asked after the people at George's office whom he had known, and then about a number of men in Philadelphia of whom George had never even heard. At last he sat back with a smile.

"Don't ever let anyone persuade you to retire, Mr. Carey," he said. "You live in the past and become a bore. A dishonest bore, too. I ask you how Harry Budd is. You tell me he's fine. What I really want to know it whether he's gone bald."

"He has," George said.

"And whether, in spite of all that studied bonhomie, he's got ulcers yet, or high blood-pressure."

George laughed.

"Because if he has," continued Mr. Moreton amiably, "that's fine. He's one son of a bitch I don't have to envy."

"Now, Bob!" his wife said reproachfully.

He spoke without looking at her, "Mr. Carey and I are going to talk a little business now, Kathy," he said.

"Very well. Don't overtire yourself."

Mr. Moreton did not reply. When she had gone, he smiled. "Drink, my boy?"

"No, thank you, sir. I think Mr. Budd explained why I wanted to see you."

"Sure. The Schneider Johnson matter. I could have guessed anyway." He looked sideways at George. "So you found it, did you?"

"Found what, sir?"

"The diary and the photographs and all Hans Schneider's stuff. You found it, eh?"

"It's outside in the car, sir, with some of your personal belongings that got put in the box with it."

Mr. Moreton nodded. "I know. I put them there myself—on top. I figured that, with any luck, a person opening the box would think that it was all just my personal junk."

"I'm afraid I don't quite follow you, sir."

"Of course you don't. I'll explain. As administrator I was ethically bound to hand over everything, lock, stock, and barrel. Well, that confidential stuff was something I didn't want to hand over. I wanted to destroy it, but Greener and Cleek wouldn't let me. They said that if anything came up afterwards and John J. found out, I'd be in trouble."

George said: "Oh." He had not really believed in his suggestion that Moreton, Greener and Cleek had concealed important information. It had merely occurred to him as a means of beguiling Mr. Budd. Now he was a trifle shocked.

Mr. Moreton shrugged. "So all I could do was to try and camouflage it. Well, I didn't succeed." He stared out gloomily at the garden for a moment, then turned to George briskly as if to dismiss an ugly memory. "I suppose the Commonwealth of Pennsylvania's after the loot again, eh?"

"Yes. They want to know if Mr. Sistrom's going to fight them on it."

"And Harry Budd, who doesn't like soiling his dainty fingers with such things, can't wait to get the thing out of the office, eh? No, you don't have to answer that, my boy. Let's get down to business."

"Would you like me to get the papers out of the car, sir?"

36

"We don't need them," said Mr. Moreton. "I know what's in that box as well as I know my own name. Did you read that little book Hans Schneider wrote for his children?"

"Yes."

"What did you think of it?"

George smiled. "After reading it I made a resolution. If I have children, I'm never going to tell them a thing about my war experiences."

The old man chuckled. "They'll get it out of you. The thing you want to watch out for is having a drip of a son like Hans who writes down what you say. That's dangerous."

"How do you mean?"

"I'll tell you. I was administrator all right, but I went to Germany because my partners sent me. Tail wagging the dog. The case had been in our hair too long and they wanted to have done with it. My instructions were to confirm what we already believed—that there was no legitimate heir to the estate. Well, when I found that Hans was probably a son of Franz Schneider's first marriage, I had to know about that marriage in order to complete the picture. As you know, I went to Potsdam to see if I could trace him through the regimental archives. To begin with, I failed."

"But next day you went back for another check through."

"Yes, but I'd had a night to think. And I'd thought again about what Hans had written. If there was any truth in the thing at all, Sergeant Schneider had become a casualty at the Battle of Eylau and been lost in the retreat. Surely the war diary would record that fact in a casualty list. So that next day, instead of going all over the nominal rolls again, I got the interpreter to translate the regimental account of the battle for me." He sighed reminiscently. "There are some moments in life, my boy, that always feel good no matter how many times you go over them again in your mind. That was one of them. It was late in the morning and getting very warm. The interpreter was having trouble with that old writing and was stumbling over the translation of it. Then he began on the account of the long march from Eylau to Insterburg. I was only half listening. As a matter of fact, I was thinking about a bad march I'd done in Cuba during the Spanish-American War. And then something the interpreter had said made me jump right out of my skin."

He paused.

"What was that?" George asked.

Mr. Moreton smiled. "I remember the words exactly. 'During this night'—I quote from the war diary— 'Franz Schirmer, a Sergeant, left the detachment under his command, saying that he was going to succour a Dragoon who had lagged behind because of a lame horse. When morning came, Sergeant Schirmer had not rejoined his detachment. There was found to be no other man missing from it, nor any who had lagged behind. Accordingly, the name of Franz Schirmer was posted in the list of deserters."

For a moment or two there was silence. "Well?" added Mr. Moreton. "What do you think of that?"

"Schirmer, did you say?"

"That's right. Sergeant Franz Schirmer, S-c-h-i-r-m-e-r."

George laughed. "The old bastard," he said.

"Exactly."

"So all that stuff he told his son Hans about the cowardly Prussians leaving him for dead was—"

"Bull," said Mr. Moreton dryly. "But you see the implications."

"Yes. What did you do?" George asked.

"The first thing I did was to take security precautions. We'd already had trouble enough with the newspapers' finding out stuff about the case and printing it, and before I went to Germany I'd agreed on a policy with my partners. I was to keep what I was doing as secret as possible; and to make sure that I didn't get an interpreter with German newspaper contacts, I was to engage him in Paris. The other thing we'd agreed on was a cipher for confidential matters.

38

It may sound funny to you, but if you've ever had experience of—"

"I know," George said. "I saw the newspaper clippings."

"Ah. Well, I'd been sending my partners progress reports in diary form. When I found out about Schirmer, I began to use the cipher. It was a simple keyword affair, but good enough for our purpose. You see, I had visions of the newspapers' getting hold of the Schirmer name and starting another flood of claims from Schirmers, Shermans, and the rest. The final thing I did was to fire the interpreter. I said I was abandoning the inquiry and paid him off."

"Why was that?"

"Because I was going on with it and I didn't want anyone outside the firm to have a complete picture. It was just as well I did fire him, too, because later on, when the Nazis were after the estate and France was occupied, the Gestapo pulled in the second man I used, for questioning. If he'd known what the first one knew, we'd have been in a spot. I got the second one through our Paris Embassy. By the time he arrived, I'd had the war-diary entry photographed—you'll find it in the file—and was ready to move on."

"To Ansbach?"

"Yes. There I found the record of Franz Schirmer's baptism. Back in Mühlhausen again, I found the register entries for the marriage of Franz and Maria Dutka, the births of Karl and Hans, and the death of Maria. But the really important thing I found was when I went back to Münster. The boy Karl was down in the recruits' muster-roll for 1824 as Karl *Schirmer*. Franz had changed his own name but not his eldest boy's."

George thought quickly. "I suppose Franz changed his name when Mühlhausen was ceded to Prussia."

"That's what I thought. As far as the Prussians were concerned, he'd be a deserter. But I guess he just didn't trouble about Karl."

"He changed Hans's name."

"But Hans was a baby then. He'd naturally grow up a Schneider. Anyway, whatever the reason, there it was. Hans had had six brothers and five sisters. All were surnamed Schneider except one, Karl. His surname was Schirmer. All I had to do was to find out which of those persons had had children—cousins of Amelia—and whether any one of those children was alive."

"That must have been quite a job."

Mr. Moreton shrugged. "Well, it wasn't quite as bad as it sounds. Death rates were higher in the last century. Out of the eleven brothers and sisters, two boys and two girls died in a typhoid epidemic before they were twelve, and another of the girls was killed by a runaway horse when she was fifteen. That meant I had only six to worry about. Four of them I handed over to a private inquiry agent specializing in that kind of thing. The other two I looked after."

"Karl Schirmer was one of your two?"

"He was. And by the middle of July I had finished with the Schneiders. There had been children all right, but none of them had survived Amelia. So there was still no heir. The only one left to check on was Karl Schirmer."

"Did he have any children?"

"Six. He'd been apprenticed to a printer in Coblenz and married the boss's daughter. I spent from mid-July on, chasing around the towns and villages of the Rhineland. By mid-August I'd traced all but one of the six, and there was still no heir. The missing child was a son, Friedrich, born in 1863. All I knew about him was that he'd married in Dortmund in 1887, and that he was a bookkeeper. And then I had trouble with the Nazis."

"What sort of trouble?"

"Well, in the summer of 1939 any foreigner who traveled about the Rhineland asking questions, checking official records, and sending cables in cipher was bound to become suspect, but, like a dope, I hadn't thought of that. In Essen I was interviewed by the police and asked to give an account of myself. I explained as best I could and they went away, but the next day they came again. This time they had a couple

40

of Gestapo boys with them." Mr. Moreton smiled ruefully. "I don't mind telling you, my boy, I was glad I had an American passport. Still, I made them believe me in the end. The fact that I was trying to prevent the papers' knowing what I was doing helped, I think. They didn't like newspapers either. The main thing was that I managed to keep the name of Schirmer out of it. But they made trouble all the same. Within two weeks I had a cable from my partners to say that the German Embassy in Washington had notified the State Department that in future the German government would represent any German national claiming the Schneider Johnson estate, and had requested complete information about the present state of the administrator's inquiries in the matter."

"You mean the Gestapo had reported what you were doing to their Foreign Office?"

"They certainly had. That's how that phony Rudolph Schneider claim of theirs started. You have no idea how difficult it is, politically and in every other way, to challenge the validity of documents produced and attested by the government of a friendly power—I mean a power enjoying normal diplomatic relations with your own government. It's like accusing them of forging their own bank-notes."

"And what about the Schirmer side of the family, sir? Did the Nazis ever get on to that?"

"No, they didn't. You see, they didn't have Amelia's documents to help them as we did. They didn't even have the right Schneider family, but it was difficult to prove."

"And Friedrich Schirmer, Karl's son? Did you trace him?"

"Yes, my boy, I traced him all right, but I had hell's own job doing it. I got on his trail at last through a clerical employment agency in Karlsruhe. They found out for me that there had been an elderly bookkeeper named Friedrich Schirmer on their files five years previously. They'd found a job for him in a button factory at Freiburg-im-Breisgau. So I went to the button factory. There they told me that he had retired

41

three years earlier at the age of seventy and gone into a clinic at Bad Schwennheim, Bladder trouble, they said. They thought he'd probably be dead."

"And was he?"

"Yes, he was dead." Mr. Moreton looked out at the garden as if he hated it. "I don't mind telling you, my boy," he said, "that I was feeling pretty old and tired myself by then. It was the last week in August and there wasn't very much doubt, from what the radio was saying, that Europe was going to be at war within the week. I wanted to go home. I've never been the sort of man who likes being in the thick of things. Besides, I was having trouble with the interpreter. He was a Lorrainer, France was mobilizing, and he was afraid he wouldn't have time to see his wife before he was called to his regiment. It was getting difficult to buy gasoline for the car, too. I was tempted to forget about Friedrich Schirmer and get out. And yet I couldn't quite bring myself to go without just making a final check-up. Twenty-four hours more, that was all I needed."

"And so you did check up." Now that he had the facts he wanted, George was getting impatient with Mr. Moreton's reminiscences.

"Yes, I checked up. But without the interpreter. He was so darned scared that I told him to take the car, drive it to Strasbourg, and wait for me there. That was a lucky thing, too. When the Gestapo got hold of him later, he knew no more than that I'd gone to Bad Schwennheim. Real luck. I went there by train. Do you know it? It's near Triburg in Baden."

"I never got down that way."

"It's one of those scattered little resort towns—pensions, family hotels, and small villas on the edge of the fir forest. I'd found that the best person to make for on those inquiries was the priest, so I set out to find him. I could see the church—like a cuckoo clock it was, on the side of the hill—and I had just about enough German to find out from a passer-by that the priest's house was beyond it. Well, I sweated up there

42

and saw the priest. Luckily, he spoke good English. I told him the usual lies, of course—"

"Lies?"

"About its being a trifling matter, a small legacy, all that stuff. You have to play it down. If you go telling the truth on a job like that you're a dead duck. Greed! You'd be surprised what happens to perfectly sane people when they start thinking in millions. So I told the usual lies and asked the usual questions."

"And the priest said Friedrich Schirmer was dead?"

"Yes." Mr. Moreton smiled slyly. "But he also said what a pity it was that I'd come too late."

"Too late for what?"

"For the funeral."

"You mean he'd survived Amelia?"

"By over ten months."

"Had he a wife?"

"She'd been dead for sixteen years."

"Children?"

"A son named Johann. That's his photograph in the box you have. Ilse was the son's wife. Johann would be in his fifties now."

"You mean he's alive?"

"I haven't any idea, my boy," said Mr. Moreton cheerfully. "But if he is, he's certainly the Schneider Johnson heir."

George smiled. "*Was* the heir you mean, don't you, sir? As a German, he could never receive the estate. The Alien Property Custodian would vest himself with the claim."

Mr. Moreton chuckled and shook his head. "Don't be so certain, my boy. According to the priest, Friedrich spent over twenty years of his life working for a German electrical manufacturer with a plant near Schaffhausen in Switzerland. Johann was born there. Technically, he'd be Swiss."

George sat back in his chair. For a moment or two he was too confused to think clearly. Mr. Moreton's pink, puffy jowls quivered with amusement. He was pleased with the effect of his statement. George felt himself getting indignant.

43

"But where did he live?" he asked. "Where *does* he live?"

"I don't know that either. Neither did the priest. As far as I could make out, the family returned to Germany in the early twenties. But Friedrich Schirmer hadn't seen or heard from his son and daughter-in-law in years. What's more, there was nothing in the papers he left to show that they'd ever existed, barring the photograph and some things he'd said to the priest."

"Did Friedrich make a will?"

"No. He had nothing to leave worth troubling about. He had lived on a small annuity. There was scarcely enough money to bury him properly."

"But surely you made an effort to find this Johann?"

"There wasn't much I could do right then. I asked Father Weichs—that was the priest—to let me know immediately if anything was heard of or from Johann, but the war broke out three days later. I never heard any more about it."

"But when the German government claimed the estate, didn't you tell them the situation and ask them to produce Johann Schirmer?"

The old man shrugged impatiently. "Of course, if it had got to the point where they had a real chance of substantiating their Schneider claim, we'd have had to. But, as it was, it was better not to show our hand. They'd already produced a phony Schneider. What was to stop them producing a phony Johann Schirmer? Supposing they'd discovered that Johann and Ilse were dead and without heirs! Do you think they'd have admitted it? Besides, we didn't expect the war to last more than a month or two; we were thinking all the time that at any moment one of us would be able to go back to Germany and clear the whole matter up in a proper way and to our own satisfaction. Then, of course, Pearl Harbor came and that was the end of the thing as far as we were concerned."

Mr. Moreton sank back on his cushions and closed his eyes. He had had his fun. Now he was tired.

George was silent. Out of the corner of his eye he could see the second Mrs. Moreton hovering in the background. He got to his feet. "There's only one thing I'm not clear about, sir," he said hesitantly.

"Yes, my boy?"

"You said that when you handed over to Mr. Sistrom in '44 you didn't want these facts to come to his attention. Why was that?"

Slowly Mr. Moreton opened his eyes. "Early in '44," he said, "my son was murdered by the S.S. after escaping from a prisoner-of-war camp in Germany. My wife wasn't too well at the time and the shock killed her. When the time came to hand the administration over, I guess I just couldn't accept the idea of a German getting anything out of this country as a result of my efforts."

"I see."

"Not professional," the old man added disapprovingly. "Not ethical. But that's the way I felt. Now—" he shrugged and his eyes were suddenly amused again —"now all I'm wondering is what Harry Budd's going to say when you tell him the news."

"I've been wondering the same thing myself," said George.

Mr. Budd said: "Oh my God!" with great force and asked his secretary to see if Mr. Sistrom was available for consultation.

John J. Sistrom was the most senior partner in the firm (Lavater and Powell had been dead for years) and had been well thought of by the elder J. P. Morgan. A remote, portentous figure who entered and left his office by a private door, he was rarely seen except by other senior partners. George had been presented to him on joining the firm and received a perfunctory handshake. He was very old, much older than Mr. Moreton, but skinny and spry—an energetic bag of bones. He fidgeted with a gold pencil while he listened to Mr. Budd's disgusted explanation of the position.

"I see," he said at last. "Well, Harry, what do you want me to do? Retain someone else, I suppose."

"Yes, John J. I thought that someone like Lieberman might be interested."

"Maybe he would. What's the exact value of the estate now?"

Mr. Budd looked at George.

"Four million three hundred thousand, sir," George said.

Mr. Sistrom pursed his lips. "Let's see. Federal tax will account for quite a bit. Then, the thing has been held up for over seven years, so the 1943 legislation applies. That means eighty percent of what's left to the Commonwealth."

"If a claimant were to get half a million out of it, he'd be lucky," said Mr. Budd.

"Half a million free of tax is a lot of money these days, Harry."

Mr. Budd laughed. Mr. Sistrom turned to George. "What's your opinion of this Johann Schirmer's claim, young man?" he asked.

"On the face of it, sir, the claim looks sound to me. A big point in its favour would seem to be the fact that although the intestacy itself comes under the 1917 act, this Schirmer claim would satisfy the tougher provisions of the '47 act. There's no question of representation. Friedrich Schirmer was a *first* cousin *and* he survived the old lady."

Mr. Sistrom nodded. "You agree with that, Harry?"

"Oh, sure. I think Lieberman will be glad to act."

"Funny things, some of these old inheritance cases," mused Mr. Sistrom absently. "They make perspectives. A German Dragoon of Napoleon's time deserts after a battle and has to change his name. Now here we sit, over a hundred years later and four thousand miles away, wondering how to deal with a situation arising out of that old fact." He smiled vaguely. "It's an interesting case. You see, we could argue that Friedrich inherited the estate prior to the appointment of the Alien Property Custodian and that it should therefore have descended to Johann Schirmer under the German law. There have been one or two cases of German-Swiss claims against the Custodian which have succeeded. There are all sort of possibilities."

46

"And won't the papers have fun when they get hold of them!" said Mr. Budd.

"Well, they don't have to get hold of them, do they? Not for the present anyway." Mr. Sistrom seemed to have come to a decision. "I don't think you ought to be too hasty about this business, Harry," he said. "Naturally, we're not going to get involved in any newspaper nonsense, but we're in the possession of certain information that nobody else has access to. We're in a strong position. I think that before we come to any decision about who's going to act we ought at least to send someone quietly to Germany to see if this Johann Schirmer can be traced. I don't like the idea of just letting the Commonwealth take all this money because we can't be bothered to fight them. If he's dead and without issue or heir, or we can't find him, then we can think again. Maybe I'll just tell the Commonwealth the facts and leave it to them in that case. But if there is some chance that the man may be alive, no matter how slight, we should bend our effort to find him. There is no need to hand over a substantial fee to another firm for doing so. Our charge for services is made irrespective of whether we are successful or not. I see no reason for turning down the opportunity."

"But, my God, John J.—"

"It's perfectly ethical for the administrator's attorneys to endeavour to find the heir and be paid for their efforts."

"I know it's ethical, John J., but jeepers—"

"In this kind of office one can get too narrow," said Mr. Sistrom firmly. "I don't think, either, that just because we're afraid of being annoyed by a little newspaper publicity we should let the business go out of the family."

There was a silence. Mr. Budd heaved a sigh. "Well, if you put it that way, John J. But suppose this man's in the Russian zone of Germany or in jail as a war criminal?"

"Then we can think again. Now, whom will you send?"

Mr. Budd shrugged. "I'd say a good, reliable, private inquiry agent was what we needed."

"Inquiry agent!" Mr. Sistrom dropped his gold pencil. "Look, Harry, we're not going to make a million dollars out of it. Competent private inquiry agents are far too expensive for a gamble like this. No, I think I have a better idea." He turned in his chair and looked at George.

George waited with a sinking heart.

The blow came.

Mr. Sistrom smiled benevolently. "How would you like a trip to Europe, Mr. Carey?" he said.

4

TWO WEEKS later George went to Paris.

As the plane from New York banked slowly and began to lose height in preparation for the landing at Orly, he could see the city turning lazily into view beneath the port wing. He craned his head to see more of it. It was not the first time he had flown over Paris; but it was the first time he had done so as a civilian, and he was curious to see if he could still identify the once familiar landmarks. He was, besides, at the beginning of a new relationship with the place. For him it had been, successively, an area on a map, the location of an Army Air Corps headquarters establishment, a fun fair in which to spend leave periods, and a grey wilderness of streets to wander in while you sweated it out waiting for transportation home. Now it had become a foreign capital in which he had business to attend to; the point of departure for what, in a facetious moment, he had thought of as an Odyssey. Not even the knowledge that he was acting merely as an inexpensive substitute for a competent private inquiry agent could quite dispel a pleasurable feeling of anticipation.

His attitude towards the Schneider Johnson case had changed somewhat during those 'two weeks. Though he still regarded his connection with it as a misfortune, he no longer saw it as a major disaster. Several things had conspired to fortify his own good sense in the matter. There had been Mr. Budd's protest against sending so able a man on so pedestrian a mission. There had been his colleagues' blasphemously expressed conviction that, having become bored with examining claims, he had cunningly misrepresented the facts in order to get himself a free vacation. Above all, there had been Mr. Sistrom's decision to take a personal interest in the matter. Mr. Budd had crossly attributed this to vulgar greed; but George suspected that Mr. Sistrom's apparently simple desire to milk the estate while he had the chance contained elements of other and less businesslike wishes. It was fantastic, no doubt, to suggest that, in a financial matter of any kind, a partner in Lavater, Powell and Sistrom could be influenced by romantic or sentimental considerations; but, as George had already perceived, fantasy and the Schneider Johnson case had never been very far apart. Besides, the belief that a schoolboy lurked in Mr. Sistrom was somehow reassuring; and reassurance was a thing of which he now stood in need.

After a further visit to Montclair, he had set to work deciphering Mr. Moreton's diary. By the time he had completed the task and identified all the photographed documents in the deed box he was aware of an unfamiliar feeling of inadequacy and self-doubt. Münster, Mühlhausen, Karlsruhe, and Berlin—he had dropped bombs on many of the places in which Mr. Moreton had worked to piece together the history of the Schirmer family. And killed quite a few of their inhabitants, no doubt. Would he have had the patience and ingenuity to do what Mr. Moreton had done? He was inclined to doubt it. It was humiliating to be comforted by the knowledge that his own task was likely to prove simpler.

The morning after his arrival in Paris, he went to the American Embassy, established relations with the legal department there, and asked them to recommend a German-English interpreter whom they had themselves used and whose sworn depositions would later be accepted by the Orphans' Court in Philadelphia and by the Alien Property Custodian.

When returned to his hotel a letter awaited him. It was from Mr. Moreton.

MY DEAR MR. CAREY:
Thank you very much for your letter. I am, of course, very interested to hear that my old friend John Sistrom has decided to take the Schirmer inquiry further, and very pleased to know that you are to have the responsibility. I congratulate you. You must stand well with John J. to be entrusted with this job. You may be sure that no newspaper will get a word out of me on the subject. I note with pleasure your flattering intention of taking the same precautionary measures as I did to ensure secrecy. If you will permit me to give you a word of advice on the interpreter question—don't take anyone you feel you do not like personally. You will be so much together that if you do not quite like him to begin with, you will end by hating the sight of him.

As to the points in my diary on which you were not clear, I have set out my answers to your questions on a separate sheet of paper. Please remember, however, that I am relying upon my memory, which in some instances may have failed me. The answers are given "to the best of my knowledge and belief."

I have given some thought to your problem in Germany and it seems to me likely that Father Weichs, the Bad Schwennheim priest, will be among those with whom you will be getting in touch at an early stage. But when I tried to recall what I had said to you about my interview with him, it seemed to me that I had left out several important things. My diary, I know, gives only the barest facts. It was my last interview in Germany and I was in a hurry to get home. But, as you may imagine, I remember the occasion vividly. A more detailed account of it may prove of some service to you.

As I told you, he informed me of Friedrich Schirmer's death and I gave him a cautious account of my reasons for inquiring about the man. We then had some conversation which, as it concerned Johann Schirmer to some extent, I will give you as I remember it.

Father Weichs is, or was, a tall, fair man with a bony face and sharp blue eyes. No fool, I warn you. And nothing passive about him. My halting German set the muscles of his jaws twitching impatiently. Fortunately, he speaks English well, and after the courtesies were over, that was the language we used.

"I hoped you might be a relative," he said. "He spoke once of an uncle in America whom he had never seen."

"Had he no relatives here? No wife?" I asked.

"His wife died about sixteen years ago, in Schaffhausen. She was a Swiss. They had lived there for over twenty years. Their son was born there. But when she died he returned to Germany. During his last illness he used to speak of his son, Johann, but he had not seen him for many years. Johann was married and he had lived with the couple for a time, but there had been a quarrel and he had left their house."

"Where did they live?"

"In Germany, but he did not tell me where. The whole subject was very painful to him. He spoke of it only once."

"What did they quarrel about?"

Father Weichs hesitated at this question. Evidently he knew the answer to it. What he said was: "I cannot say."

"You don't know?" I persisted.

He hesitated again, then answered very carefully:

51

"Friedrich Schirmer was not, perhaps, as simple a man as he appeared. That is all I can say."

"I see."

"De mortuis . . . the old man was very sick."

"You have absolutely no idea then, Father, of the whereabouts of Johann?"

"I regret, none. I looked among the old man's things for the address of someone to tell of his death, but I did not find anything. He lived at the sanatorium for old people. The woman director there said that he received no letters, only his annuity every month. Will the son receive the legacy now?"

I had been prepared for the question. At one moment I had thought of trusting this priest, but the habit of caution was very strong. I answered evasively. "The money is in trust," I said, and changed the subject by asking what had happened to his belongings.

"There was little more than the clothes he was buried in," he said.

"No will?"

"No. There were a few books and some old papers—records of his army service, such things. Nothing of value. I have charge of them until the authorities tell me they may be destroyed."

Naturally, I was determined to go through these things myself, but tact was necessary. "I wonder if I might see them, Father," I said. "It would be fitting, perhaps, if I could tell his relatives in America that I had done so."

"Certainly, if you wish."

He had made a package of the papers and put the dead man's rosary in with them. I looked through them.

It was, I must tell you, a pathetic collection. There were old Swiss concert programs and catalogues of Swiss electrical trade exhibitions, an accountancy diploma from a commercial college in Dortmund, and the autographed menu of a banquet held in 1910 for the German employees of the Schaffhausen plant he had worked in. There were letters from business houses all over Germany replying to applications for book-

keeping posts. Dates from 1927 and on. The applicant had written from Dortmund, Mainz, Hanover, Karlsruhe and Freiburg, in that date order. There were the army papers and the documents connected with the annuity he had purchased with his savings. In expansive moments I have been known to contend that the apparently unimportant things a man keeps, the private souvenirs, the clutter he . accumulates during his lifetime, are an index to the secrets of his soul. If this is so, then Friedrich Schirmer must have led a singularly uneventful inner life.

There were two photographs—the one you have seen of Johann and Ilse and another of the late Frau (Friedrich) Schirmer. I knew that I must have the one of Johann at all costs. I put them down casually.

"Nothing of interest, you see," said Father Weichs.

I nodded. "But," I said, "I wonder if it would not be a kindly action for me to take some remembrance of him back to his relatives in America. If these things are to be destroyed, it seems a pity not to save something of him."

He thought for a moment but could see no objection. He suggested the rosary. I immediately agreed and only brought up the matter of the photograph as an afterthought. "If, by any chance, it should be wanted, I could always copy it and return the original to you," I said.

So I took it with me. I also had his promise that in the event of his learning anything of the whereabouts of Johann Schirmer, I should be informed. As you know, I have never heard from him. In the early hours of the following day, the German army crossed the frontier and began to advance into Poland.

Well, there it is, my boy. My wife has been good enough to type it all out for me and I hope it will be of some use to you. If there is anything else I can do, let me know. And if you feel that you can, without betraying your firm's confidence, let me know how you get on, I shall be more than pleased to hear. You know, the only one of all the Schneiders and Schirmers I got to know about that I really liked was that old

53

Sergeant Franz. I imagine that he was quite a tough proposition. What happens to blood like that? Oh yes, I know that only certain physical characteristics get transmitted, and that it's all a matter of genes and chromosomes; but if you do happen to run across a Schirmer with a beard like Franz's, let me know. Good luck anyway.

Sincerely,

ROBERT L. MORETON

George refolded the letter and looked at the accompanying sheet of paper with the answer to his questions. As he did so, the telephone by his bed buzzed harshly and he turned to answer it.

"Mademoiselle Kolin to see you, sir."

"All right. I'll come down."

This was the interpreter who had been recommended to him by the Embassy.

"Miss Kolin?" George had said. "A woman?"

"Sure, she's a woman."

"I assumed you'd get a man. You know I've got to travel all over the place staying at hotels. It's going to be awkward if—"

"Why? You don't have to sleep with her."

"Isn't there a man available?"

"Not as good as Miss Kolin. You said you wanted someone we could vouch for if it came to getting the interpreter's testimony accepted in an American court. We could vouch for Kolin all right. We always use her or Miss Harle for important rogatory commissions, and so do the British. Harle's on another job in Geneva right now, so we got Kolin. You're lucky she's available."

"All right. How old is she?"

"Early thirties and quite attractive."

"For God's sake."

"You don't have to worry." The Embassy man had chuckled in an odd way.

George had ignored the chuckle and asked about Miss Kolin's history.

She had been born in one of the Serbian towns of

Yugoslavia and was a graduate of the University of Belgrade. She had an almost phenomenal talent for languages. A British Major working with a relief organization had found her in a displaced-persons camp in 1945 and employed her as a secretary. Later she had worked as an interpreter for an American legal team doing preparatory work for the Nuremberg trials. When the team's work had ended, one of the lawyers, impressed as much by her secretarial ability as by the fact that she was multilingual, had given her introductions to the International Standards Organization and the American Embassy in Paris and advised her to try to work up a connection as an interpreter and verbatim reporter. She had soon established herself. She now had a solid reputation at international trade conferences for the speed and reliability of her work. Her services were much in demand.

There were several women waiting in the foyer of the hotel and George had to ask the concierge to point his visitor out to him.

Maria Kolin was indeed attractive. She had the sort of figure and posture that makes inexpensive clothes look good. The face and features were broad, the complexion brown against sleek straw-coloured hair. Her eyes were prominent and heavy-lidded. The only make-up she wore was lipstick, but this was boldly applied. She looked as if she had just returned from a ski-ing holiday.

Although she had obviously seen the concierge point her out to him, she remained staring blankly into the middle distance as George approached, and gave an unreal start of surprise when he spoke.

"Miss Kolin? I'm George Carey."

"How do you do?" She touched the hand he held out to her as if it were a rolled-up newspaper.

"I'm very glad you could come along," George said.

She shrugged stiffly. "Naturally, you would wish to interview me before deciding to employ me." Her English was very clear and precise, with only the faintest trace of an accent.

"They told me at the Embassy that you were a busy person and that I was lucky you were available." He put as much friendliness as he could into his smile.

She looked past him vaguely. "Ah, yes?"

George felt himself beginning to be irritated by her. "Shall we sit down somewhere and talk, Miss Kolin?"

"Of course."

He led the way across the foyer to some comfortable chairs near the bar. She followed a little too slowly. His irritation increased. She might be an attractive woman, but there was no reason for her to behave as if she were fending off a clumsy attempt at seduction. She was here about a job. Did she want it or didn't she? If she didn't, why waste time by coming at all?

"Now, Miss Kolin," he said as they sat down, "how much did the Embassy people tell you about this job?

"That you were going to Germany to interview various persons there in connection with a lawsuit. That you would want verbatim reports of the interviews transcribed. That it might be necessary to attend later at an American Embassy to have these transcriptions notarized. The length of time for which you would require me would be not less than one month and not more than three. I should receive my normal fees on a monthly basis, and all travelling and hotel expenses would be paid in addition." She looked past him again, her head held high—a lady of quality importuned by a lascivious workman.

"Yes, that's about right," George said. "Did they tell you which lawsuit it was?"

"They said that it was a highly confidential matter and that you would no doubt explain what it was necessary for me to know." A faint, indifferent smile —men are such children with their little secrets.

"Right. What passport do you have, Miss Kolin?"

"French."

"I understood you were a Yugoslav citizen."

"I am naturalized French. My passport *is* valid for Germany."

"Yes, that was what I wanted to know."

She nodded but did not say anything. One would be patient with the slow-witted, but one was not obliged to pander to them.

Several sentences came to the tip of George's tongue at that moment, most of them designed to bring the interview to an abrupt conclusion. He swallowed them. Just because she wouldn't pretend to be stupider or more eager for the work than she really was, he didn't have to insult the woman. She had an unfortunate manner. All right! Did that make her a bad interpreter? And what did he expect her to do? Cringe?

He offered her a cigarette.

She shook her head. "Thank you. I prefer these." She brought out a packet of Gitanes.

He struck a match for her. "Are there any questions about the job you would like to ask me?" he said.

"Yes." She blew smoke out. "Have you had any experience of using an interpreter, Mr. Carey?"

"None at all."

"I see. Do you speak any German?"

"A little, yes."

"How little? It is not a pointless question."

"I'm sure it isn't. Well, I speak the German I learned at high school. I was stationed in Germany for a few months after the war and heard a fair amount of German spoken there. I can understand the drift of most conversations between Germans, but I sometimes misunderstand so completely that I might think I was listening to an argument about politics when what I was really hearing was a discussion of the finer points of chicken farming. Does that answer your question?"

"Very clearly. I will explain the point. When you are using an interpreter, it is not always easy to avoid listening also to the conversation being interpreted. That way confusion may arise."

"In fact, it's better to trust to the interpreter and not try to do the work for her."

"Exactly."

The barman was hovering in the background. George ignored him. The interview was as good as over and he did not want to prolong it. Her cigarette was half smoked now. When it had burned down another quarter of an inch, he would get up.

"I expect you know Germany pretty well, Miss Kolin."

"Only certain parts."

"The Rhineland?"

"A little."

"You worked on the preparations for the Nuremberg trials, I hear."

"Yes."

"As a Yugoslav you must have found that very satisfactory."

"You think so, Mr. Carey?"

"You didn't approve of the trials?"

She looked down at her cigarette. "The Germans took my father as a hostage and shot him," she said crisply. "They sent my mother and me to work in a factory in Leipzig. My mother died there of blood-poisoning from an infected wound which they refused to treat. I do not know exactly what happened to my brothers, except that eventually they were tortured to death in an S.S. barracks at Zagreb. Oh yes, I approved of the trials. If they made the United Nations feel strong and righteous, certainly I approved. But do not ask me to applaud."

"Yes, I can see you must have wished for a more personal revenge."

She had leaned forward to stub her cigarette out. Now she turned her head slowly and her eyes met his.

"I'm afraid that I have not your belief in justice, Mr. Carey," she said.

There was a curious, persecuted little half-smile on her lips. He realized suddenly that he was on the verge of losing his temper.

She rose to her feet and stood in front of him smoothing down her dress. "Is there anything else you would like to know?" she asked calmly.

"I don't think so, thank you." He stood up. "It was very kind of you to come along, Miss Kolin. I'm not sure yet when I shall be leaving Paris. I'll get in touch with you as soon as I know."

"Of course." She picked up her bag. "Good-bye, Mr. Carey."

"Good afternoon, Miss Kolin."

With a nod she went.

For a moment he looked down at the cigarette she had stubbed out and the lipstick on it; then he went to the lift and was taken up to his room.

He telephoned the Embassy man immediately.

"I've just seen Miss Kolin," he said.

"Good. All fixed up?"

"No, *not* all fixed up. Look, Don, isn't there somebody else I can get?"

"What's the matter with Kolin?"

"I don't know, but whatever it is I don't like it."

"You must have caught one of her bad days. I told you she'd had some pretty rugged experiences as a refugee."

"Look, I've talked to lots of refugees who've had rugged experiences. I've never talked to one before who made me sympathize with the Gestapo."

"Too bad. Her work's O.K., though."

"She's not."

"You wanted the best interpreter available."

"I'll take the next best."

"Nobody who's actually worked with Kolin has ever had anything but praise for her."

"She may be fine for conferences and committees. This is different."

"What's different about it? You're not on a vacation trip are you?" There was a note of irritation in the voice now.

George hesitated. "No, but—"

"Supposing there's a dispute later over the testimony. You're going to look pretty silly explaining that you passed up the chance of getting a reliable interpreter because you didn't like her personality, aren't you, George?"

"Well—" George broke off and then sighed. "O.K.

—if I come back a raving alcoholic I shall send the doctor's bills to you."

"You'll probably end by marrying the girl."

George laughed politely and hung up.

Two days later he and Maria Kolin left for Germany.

5

A BOOK-KEEPER named Friedrich Schirmer had died at Bad Schwennheim in 1939. He had a son named Johann. Find this son. If he was dead, then find his heir.

Those were George's instructions.

There were probably thousands of Johann Schirmers in Germany, but certain things were known about this one. He had been born somewhere about 1895, in Schaffhausen. He had married a woman whose given name was Ilse. There was a photograph of the two taken in the early twenties. George had a copy. It would probably be of little help in making a positive identification at this stage, but it might serve to remind former neighbours or acquaintances of the pair. Appearances were usually better remembered than names. The photograph itself supplied another faint clue; the photographer's imprint on the mount showed that it had been taken in Zurich.

However, the first move in the plan of campaign which Mr. Sistrom had mapped out for him was, as Mr. Moreton had surmised, to go to Bad Schwennheim and start where the former inquiry had stopped.

When Friedrich Schirmer had died, he had been estranged from his son for several years; but there was always a chance that the war might have changed things. Families tended to draw together in emergencies.

It would have been natural, Mr. Sistrom had contended, for Johann to try to get in touch with his father at that time. If he had done so, he would have been officially notified of the death. There might be a record of that notification giving his address. True, Mr. Moreton had heard nothing on the subject from Bad Schwennheim, but that proved nothing. The priest might have forgotten his promise or neglected it; his letter could have been lost in the uncertain war-time mails; he might have gone off into the German army as a chaplain. There were endless possibilities.

In the train on the way to Basel, George explained it all to Miss Kolin.

She listened attentively. When he had finished she nodded. "Yes, I see. You can, of course, neglect no possibility." She paused. "Do you hope much from Bad Schwennheim, Mr. Carey?"

"Not much, no. I don't know exactly what the German procedure is, but I would say that when an old man like this Friedrich dies, the authorities don't fall over backwards finding relations to notify. We wouldn't, anyway. What's the point? There's no estate. And supposing Johann did write. The letter would go to the sanatorium and most likely get returned through the mail marked 'Addressee deceased' or whatever it is they put. The priest could easily not have heard about it."

She pursed her lips. "It is curious about this old man."

"Not very. That sort of thing happens every day, you know."

"You say that Mr. Moreton found nothing of the son except this one photograph among the old man's papers. No letters, no other photographs, except of his dead wife, nothing. They quarrelled, we are told. It would be interesting to know why."

"The wife got tired of having him around, probably."

"What disease did he die of?"

"Bladder trouble of some sort."

"He would know he was dying, and yet he did not

61

write to his son before the end or even ask the priest to do so?"

"Perhaps he just didn't care any more."

"Perhaps." She thought for a moment. "Do you know the name of the priest?"

"It was a Father Weichs."

"Then I think you could make inquiries before going to Bad Schwennheim. You could find out if Father Weichs is still there from the church authorities at Freiburg. If he is not still there, they will be able to tell you where he is. You might save much time that way."

"That's a good idea, Miss Kolin."

"At Freiburg you may also be able to find out if the old man's belongings were claimed by a relative."

"I think we may have to go to Baden for that information, but we can try at Freiburg."

"You do not object that I make these suggestions, Mr. Carey?"

"Not a bit. On the contrary, they're very helpful."

"Thank you."

George did not find it necessary to mention that the ideas she had put forward had, in fact, already occurred to him. He had given some thought to Miss Kolin since making his reluctant decision to employ her.

He disliked her and, if Mr. Moreton were to be believed, would end by detesting her. She was not somebody he had chosen freely to serve him. She had, to all intents and purposes, been imposed upon him. It would be senseless, therefore, to behave towards her as if she ought to represent—as a good secretary ought to represent, for instance—an extension of part of his own mind and will. She was rather more in the position of an unsympathetic associate with whom it was his duty to collaborate amicably until a specific piece of work was done. He had encountered and dealt philosophically with such situations in the army; there was no reason why he should not deal philosophically with this one.

Thus, having prepared himself for the worst, he had found the Miss Kolin who had presented herself with suitcase and portable typewriter at the Gare de l'Est that morning an agreeable modification of it. True, she had marched along the platform as if she were going out to face a firing-squad, and, true, she looked as if she had been insulted several times already that day, but she had greeted him in quite a friendly fashion and had then disconcerted him by producing an excellent map of Western Germany on which she had drawn for his convenience the boundaries of the various occupation zones. She had accepted with businesslike comprehension his patently guarded outline of the case, and shown herself alert and practical when he had gone on to explain in detail the nature of the work they had to do in Germany. Now she was making intelligent and helpful suggestions. Kolin on the job was evidently a very different person from Kolin being interviewed for one. Or perhaps the man at the Embassy had been right and, having experienced one of her bad days, he was now enjoying a good one. In that case it would be as well to discover how, if at all, the bad might be avoided. In the meantime he could hope.

After two good days in Freiburg, his attitude towards his collaborator had undergone a further change. He was no nearer liking her, but he had acquired a respect for her ability which, from a professional standpoint at any rate, was far more comforting. Within two hours of their arrival, she had discovered that Father Weichs had left Bad Schwennheim in 1943, having been called to the Hospital of the Sacred Heart, an institution for disabled men and women, just outside Stuttgart. By the end of the following day she had unearthed the facts that Friedrich Schirmer's belongings had been disposed of under a law dealing with the intestacy of paupers and that the dead man's next of kin was recorded as "Johann Schirmer, son, whereabouts unknown."

To begin with he had attempted to direct each step of the inquiry himself, but as they were passed from one official to another, the laborious time-wasting routine of question and interpretation followed by answer and interpretation became absurd. At his suggestion she began to interpret the substance of conversations. Then, in the middle of one interview, she had broken off impatiently.

"This is not the person you want," she had told him. "You will waste time here. There is, I think, a simpler way."

After that he had stood back and let her go ahead. She had done so with considerable energy and self-assurance. Her methods of dealing with people were artless but effective. With the co-operative she was brisk, with the obstructive she was imperious, for the suspicious she had a bright, metallic smile. In America, George decided, the smile would not have beguiled an oversexed schoolboy; but in Germany it seemed to work. Its final triumph was the persuasion of a dour functionary in the police department to telephone to Baden-Baden for the court records of the disposal of Friedrich Schirmer's estate.

It was all very satisfactory, and George said so as handsomely as he could.

She shrugged. "It does not seem necessary for you to waste your time with these simple, routine inquiries. If you feel you can trust me to take care of them I am glad to do so."

It was that evening that he found out something rather more disconcerting about Miss Kolin.

They had fallen into the habit of discussing the next day's work briefly over dinner. Afterwards she would go to her room and George would write letters or read. This particular evening, however, they had been drawn into conversation with a Swiss businessman in the bar before dinner and were later invited by him to sit at his table. His motive was quite evidently the seduction of Miss Kolin, if that could be accomplished without too much trouble and if George had no objection. George had none. The man was agreeable and spoke good English; George was interested to see how he would make out.

Miss Kolin had had four brandies before dinner. The Swiss had had several Pernods. With dinner she drank wine. So did the Swiss. After dinner he invited her to have brandy again, and again ordered large ones. She had four. So did the Swiss. With the second of them he became coyly amorous and tried to stroke her knee. She repelled the advance absently but efficiently. By the time he had finished his third, he was haranguing George bitterly on the subject of American fiscal policies. Shortly after his fourth he went very pale, excused himself hurriedly, and did not reappear. With a nod to the waiter Miss Kolin ordered a fifth for herself.

George had noticed on previous evenings that she liked brandy and that she rarely ordered anything else to drink. He had even noticed when they had been going through the customs in Basel that she carried a bottle of it in her suitcase. He had not, however, observed that it affected her in any way. Had he been questioned on the point he would have said that she was a model of sobriety.

Now, as she sipped the new arrival, he watched her, fascinated. He knew that had he been drinking level with her, he would by now have been unconscious. She was not even talkative. She was holding herself very upright in the chair and looking like an attractive but very prudish young schoolmistress about to deal for the first time with a case of juvenile exhibitionism. There was a suspicion of drool at one corner of her mouth. She retrieved it neatly with her tongue. Her eyes were glassy. She focused them with care on George.

"We go then, tomorrow to the sanatorium at Bad Schwennheim?" she said precisely.

"No, I don't think so. We'll go and see Father Weichs at Stuttgart first. If he knows something it may be unnecessary to go to Bad Schwennheim."

She nodded. "I think you are right, Mr. Carey."

She looked at her drink for a moment, finished it at a gulp, and rose steadily to her feet.

"Good night, Mr. Carey," she said firmly.

"Good night, Miss Kolin."

She picked up her bag, turned round, and positioned

herself facing the door. Then she began to walk straight for it. She missed a table by a hairsbreadth. She did not sway. She did not teeter. It was a miraculous piece of self-control. George saw her go out of the restaurant, change direction towards the concierge's desk, pick up her room key, and disappear up the stairs. To a casual observer she might have had nothing stronger to drink than a glass of Rhine wine.

The Hospital of the Sacred Heart proved to be a grim brick building some way out of Stuttgart off the road to Heilbronn.

George had taken the precaution of sending a long telegram to Father Weichs. In it he had recalled Mr. Moreton's visit to Bad Schwennheim in 1939 and expressed his own wish to make the priest's acquaintance. He and Miss Kolin were kept waiting for only a few minutes before a nun appeared to guide them through a wilderness of stone corridors to the priest's room.

George remembered that Father Weichs spoke good English, but it seemed more tactful to begin in German. The priest's sharp blue eyes flickered from one to the other of them as Miss Kolin translated George's polite explanation of their presence there and his hope that the telegram (which he could plainly see on the priest's table) had arrived to remind him of an occasion in 1939 when . . .

The muscles of Father Weichs's jaws had been twitching impatiently as he listened. Now he broke in, speaking English.

"Yes, Mr. Carey. I remember the gentleman, and, as you see, I have had your telegram. Please sit down." He waved them to chairs and walked back to his table.

"Yes," he said, "I remember the gentleman very well. I had reason to."

A twisted smile creased the lean cheeks. It was a fine, dramatic head, George thought. You were sure at first that he must hold some high office in the church; and then you noticed the cracked, clumsy shoes beneath the table, and the illusion went.

"He asked me to give you his good wishes," George said.

"Thank you. Are you here on his behalf?"

"Unfortunately, Mr. Moreton is now an invalid and retired." It was difficult not to be stilted with Father Weichs.

"I am sorry to hear that, of course." The priest inclined his head courteously. "However, it was not the gentleman himself who gave me special cause to remember him. Consider! A lonely old man dies. I am his confessor. Mr. Moreton comes to me asking questions about him. That is all. It is not as unusual as you think. An old person who has been neglected by relatives for many years often becomes interesting to them when he dies. It is not often, of course, that an American lawyer comes, but even that is not remarkable in itself. There are many German families who have ties with your country." He paused. "But the incident becomes memorable," he added dryly, "when it proves to be a matter of importance for the police."

"The police?" George tried hard not to look as guilty as he suddenly felt.

"I surprise you, Mr. Carey?"

"Very much. Mr. Moreton was making inquiries on behalf of a perfectly respectable American client in the matter of a legacy—" George began.

"A legacy," interposed the priest, "which he said was for a small amount of money." He paused and gave George a wintry smile before he went on. "I understand, of course, that size is relative and that in America it is not measured with European scales, but even in America it seems an exaggeration to call three million dollars a small amount."

Out of the corner of his eye George saw Miss Kolin looking startled for once; but it was a poor satisfaction at that moment.

"Mr. Moreton was in a spot, Father," he said. "He had to be discreet. The American papers had already caused trouble by giving the case too much publicity. There had been a whole lot of false claims. Besides, the case was very complicated. Mr. Moreton didn't

67

want to raise anybody's hopes and then have to disappoint them."

The priest frowned. "His discretion placed me in a very dangerous position with the police. And with certain other authorities," he added bleakly.

"I see. I'm sorry about that, Father. I think if Mr. Moreton had known—" He broke off. "Do you mind telling me what happened?"

"If it is of interest to you. A little before Christmas in 1940 the police came to me to ask questions about Mr. Moreton's visit of the year before. I told them what I knew. They wrote it down and went away. Two weeks later they came back with some other men, not of the police, but the Gestapo. They took me to Karlsruhe." His face hardened. "They accused me of lying about Mr. Moreton's visit. They said that it was a matter of highest importance to the Reich. They said that if I did not tell them what they wished to know, I would be treated as some of my brothers in the church had been treated." He had been looking at his hands. Now he raised his head, and his eyes met George's. "Perhaps you are able to guess what they wanted to know, Mr. Carey."

George cleared his throat. "I should say they wanted to know about someone named Schneider."

He nodded. "Yes, someone named Schneider. They said that Mr. Moreton had been searching for this person and that I was concealing my knowledge. They believed that I knew where this person was who was entitled to the American money and that Mr. Moreton had bought my silence so that the money could go to an American." He shrugged. "The sadness of evil men is that they can believe no truth that does not paint the world in their colours."

"They weren't interested in Friedrich Schirmer?"

"No. I think that they believed in the end that it was a trick of Mr. Moreton's to mislead them. I do not know. Perhaps they only became tired of me. In any case, they let me go. But you see I have reason to remember Mr. Moreton."

"Yes. But I don't see how he could have anticipated the trouble he would cause you."

"Oh, I have no bitterness, Mr. Carey." He sat back in his chair. "But I should like to know the truth."

George hesitated. "Friedrich Schirmer's family was a branch of the Schneider family in question. The actual connection would take a long time to explain, but I can tell you that the German government did not know of it."

The priest smiled. "I see that it is still necessary to be discreet."

George flushed. "I'm being as frank as I can, Father. This has always been a pretty funny sort of a case. There have been so many false claimants to the estate already that, even if a legitimate one were found, it would be enormously difficult now to establish the claim in the American courts. The fact is that, in all probability, no claim ever will be established. The money will just go to the Commonwealth of Pennsylvania."

"Then why are you here, Mr. Carey?"

"Partly because the law firm I work for succeeded Mr. Moreton in the matter. Partly because it is our duty to find the heir. Partly because the matter has to be cleared up so that our firm may be paid."

"That, at least, is frank."

"Maybe I should add, too, that if there *is* a rightful heir, then he or she ought to have the money and not the Commonwealth of Pennsylvania. The federal government and the state will get most of it in taxes in the end anyway, but there's no reason why someone else shouldn't enjoy it too."

"Mr. Moreton mentioned a trust."

"Well—"

"Ah, I see. That also was discretion."

"I'm afraid so."

"Was Friedrich Schirmer the rightful heir?"

"Mr. Moreton thought so."

"Then why did Mr. Moreton not tell the courts so?"

"Because Friedrich Schirmer was dead and because he was afraid that if Friedrich were found to have no living heir, the German government would fake one to get the money. In fact they did produce an old man they claimed to be the heir. Mr. Moreton fought the claim for over a year."

Father Weichs was silent for a moment; then he sighed. "Very well. How can I help you now, Mr. Carey?"

"Mr. Moreton said that you promised to let him know if Friedrich Schirmer's son, Johann, appeared. Did he?"

"No."

"Do you know if any letters ever came for Friedrich Schirmer to the sanatorium where he died?"

"Up to the middle of 1940 no letter came."

"You would have known?"

"Oh yes. I visited the sanatorium often."

"And after the middle of 1940?"

"The sanatorium was commandeered by the army. It became the headquarters of a training school for radio operators."

"I see. Well, that seems to be fairly conclusive." George stood up. "Thanks a lot, Father."

But Father Weichs had made a movement of protest. "One moment, Mr. Carey. You asked if Johann Schirmer came to Bad Schwennheim."

"Yes?"

"He did not come, but his son did."

"His son?" Slowly George sat down again.

"He would be of interest to you, the son?"

"If he were a grandson of Friedrich Schirmer, he would interest me very much."

Father Weichs nodded. "He came to see me. I must explain that when the army occupied the sanatorium, I visited the Commandant of the school to offer the services of my church to those who wished them. The Commandant was not himself of the religion, but he was sympathetic and made it as easy as possible for those who wished to come to Mass."

He looked thoughtful at George. "I do not know if you served in the army, Mr. Carey," he went on after a moment or two. George nodded. "So! Then you may have noticed that there were some men—among the young front fighters I mean—who were not religious and yet found it necessary sometimes to seek some of the consolations of religion. It was when they had to find the courage to face death or mutilation, after they had seen what those things were, that the need seemed to come. Then the elaborate materialism of the intelligent among them proved as useless and sterile as the hero myths they had brought with them from the Hitler *Jugend*. They found that they needed something else, and sometimes they went to a priest to look for it." He smiled faintly. "Of course, it never appeared as simple as that at the time. They came to me for many commonplace reasons, these young men—to talk about their families, to ask advice on some material problem, to borrow a book or a magazine, to show photographs they had taken, to enjoy the privacy of a garden. But the outward reason was unimportant. Though they might not always realize it, what they wanted was, in some way, to come to terms with me as a priest. They wanted something that in their hearts they thought I might be able to give them —an inner peace and strength."

"And Schirmer's grandson was one of them?"

Father Weichs shrugged. "I was not sure. Perhaps, yes. But I will tell you. He had been sent to the school for special training. He was a—"

He broke off, hesitating, and then, glancing at Miss Kolin, said the word *Fallschirmjäger*.

"He was a paratrooper," she said.

The priest nodded. "Thank you, yes. He came to see me one day in September or October—I do not quite remember. He was a tall, strong-looking young man, very much a soldier. He had been wounded in Belgium in the attack on the fortress of Eben-Emael, and was not yet well enough to return to combat duty. He came to ask me if I knew of his grandfather, Friedrich Schirmer."

"Did he say where his home was?" asked George quickly.

"Yes. He came from Köln."

71

"Did he say what his father's occupation was?"

"No. I cannot remember that he did."

"Had he any brothers or sisters?"

"No, he was the only child."

"Did he know when he came that his grandfather was dead?"

"No. It was a great disappointment to him. When he was a boy the grandfather had lived in his parents' house and been kind to him. Then one day there had been a quarrel and the old man had gone."

"Did he say how he knew that the old man had lived at Bad Schwennheim?"

"Yes. The quarrel had been serious, and after Friedrich left, his name was never mentioned by the boy's parents. But the boy loved his grandfather. Even before he went to school the old man had taught him how to write and rule his exercise books properly. Later the grandfather helped him with arithmetic problems and talked to him much of commercial affairs. You knew Friedrich Schirmer was a bookkeeper?"

"Yes."

"The boy did not forget him. When he was about fourteen his parents received a letter from the old man saying that he was retiring to live at Bad Schwennheim. He had heard them discussing it. They destroyed the letter, but he remembered the name of the town, and when he was sent to the army school there he tried to find his grandfather. He did not know until I told him that, by a strange chance, he was living in the building where the old man had died."

"I see."

Father Weichs looked down at his hands. "You would not have thought to see him or speak with him that he was a young man whom it was necessary to protect from disillusion. I think I failed him. I did not understand him until it was too late. He came to see me several times. He asked many questions about his grandfather. I saw afterwards that he wanted to make a hero of him. At the time I did not think. I answered the questions as kindly as I could. Then one day he asked me if I did not think that his grandfather Friedrich had been a fine and good man." He paused and then went on slowly and carefully as if choosing words in his own defense. "I made the best answer I could. I said that Friedrich Schirmer had been a hard-working man and that he had suffered his long, painful illness with patience and courage. I could say no more. The boy took my words for agreement and began to speak with great bitterness of his father, who had, he said, sent the old man away in a moment of jealous hatred. I could not allow him to speak so. It was against the truth. I said that he was doing his father a great injustice, that he should go to his father and ask for the truth." He raised his eyes and looked at George sombrely. "He laughed. He said that he had never yet had anything from his father that was good and would not get the truth. He went on to talk jokingly of his father as if he despised him. Then he went away. I did not see him again."

Outside, on the iron balconies of the hospital, the shadows were getting longer. A clock tolled the hour.

"And what *was* the truth, Father?" asked George quietly.

The priest shook his head. "I was Friedrich Schirmer's confessor, Mr. Carey."

"Of course. I'm sorry."

"It would not help you to know."

"No, I see that. But tell me this, Father. Mr. Moreton made a rough list of the documents and photographs that were found after Friedrich Schirmer's death. Was that all he had? Was nothing else ever found?"

To his surprise, he saw a look of embarrassment come over the priest's face. His eyes avoided George's. For a moment or two there was something positively furtive about Father Weichs's expression.

"Old documents," George added quickly, "can be very important evidence in cases like these."

Father Weichs's jaw muscles tightened. "There were no other documents," he said.

"Or photographs?"

73

"None that could possibly have been of any value to you, Mr. Carey," the priest replied stiffly.

"But there *were* other photographs?" George insisted.

Father Weichs's jaw muscles began to twitch. "I repeat, Mr. Carey, that they would have had no bearing on your inquiry," he said.

" '*Would* have had'?" George echoed. "Do you mean they no longer exist, Father?"

"I do. They no longer exist. I burned them."

"I see," said George.

There was a heavy silence while they looked at one another. Then Father Weichs got to his feet with a sigh and looked out of the window.

"Friedrich Schirmer was not a pleasant man," he said at last. "I see no harm in telling you that. You may even have guessed from what I have already said. There were many of these photographs. They were never of importance to anyone but Friedrich Schirmer —and possibly to those from whom he bought them."

George understood. "Oh," he said blankly. "Oh, I see." He smiled. He had a strong desire to laugh.

"He had made his peace with God," said Father Weichs. "It seemed kinder to destroy them. The secret lusts of the dead should end with the flesh that created them. Besides," he added briskly, "there is always the risk of such erotica getting into the hands of children."

George got to his feet. "Thanks, Father. There are just a couple more things I'd like to ask you. Did you ever know what unit of the paratroopers young Schirmer was serving in?"

"No. I regret that I did not."

"Well, we can find that out later. What were his given names, Father, and his rank? Do you remember?"

"I only knew one name. Franz, it was, I think. Franz Schirmer. He was a Sergeant."

6

THEY STAYED that night in Stuttgart. Over dinner George summed up the results of their work.

"We can go straight to Cologne and try to find the Johann Schirmers by going through the city records," he went on; "or we can go after the German army records, turn up Franz Schirmer's papers, and get hold of his parents' address that way."

"Why should the army have his parents' address?"

"Well, if it were our army he'd been in, his personal file would probably show the address of his parents, or wife if he's married, as next of kin. Someone they can notify when you've been killed is a thing most armies like to have. What do you think?"

"Cologne is a big city—nearly a million persons before the war. But I have not been there."

"I have. It was a mess when I saw it. What the R.A.F. didn't do to it our army did. I don't know whether the city archives were saved or not, but I'm inclined to go for the army records first just in case."

"Very well."

"In fact, I think the army is a better bet all around. Two birds with one stone. We'll find out what happened to Sergeant Schirmer at the same time as we trace his parents. Do you have any ideas about where his German army records would be?"

"Bonn is the West German capital. Logically they should be there now."

"But you don't really think they will be, eh? Neither do I. Anyway I think we'll go to Frankfurt tomorrow. I can check up with the American army people there. They'll know. Another brandy?"

"Thank you."

A further thing he had discovered about Miss Kolin was that, although she probably consumed, in public or in the privacy of her room, over half a bottle of brandy every day, she did not seem to suffer from hangovers.

It took them nearly two weeks to find out what the German army knew about Sergeant Schirmer.

He had been born in Winterthur in 1917, the son of Johann Schirmer (mechanic) and Ilse, his wife, both of pure German stock. From the Hitler *Jugend* he had joined the army at the age of eighteen and been promoted corporal in 1937. He had been transferred from the Engineers to a special air training unit (*Fallschirmjäger*) in 1938 and promoted sergeant in the following year. At Eben-Emael he had received a bullet wound in the shoulder, from which he had satisfactorily recovered. He had taken part in the invasion of Crete and had been awarded the Iron Cross (Third Class) for distinguished conduct. In Benghazi later in that year he had suffered from dysentery and malaria. In Italy in 1943, while acting as a parachutist instructor, he had fractured a hip. There had been a court of inquiry to determine who had been responsible for giving the order to jump over wooded country. The court had commended the Sergeant's conduct in refraining from transmitting an order he believed to be incorrect, while obeying it himself. After four months in hospital and at a rehabilitation centre, and a further period of sick leave, a medical board had declared him unfit for further duty as a paratrooper or any other combat duty which entailed excessive marching. He had been posted to the occupation forces in Greece. There, he had served as a weapons instructor for the Ninety-fourth Garrison Regiment in a Lines of Communication Division stationed in the Salonika area, until the following year. After an action against Greek guerrillas during the withdrawal from Macedonia, he had been reported "missing, believed killed." The next of kin, Ilse

76

Schirmer, Elsass Str. 39, Köln, had been duly notified.

They found Elsass Strasse, or what was left of it, in the remains of the old town off the Neumarkt.

Before the stick of bombs which had destroyed it had fallen, it had been a narrow street of small shops with offices above them, and a tobacco warehouse half-way along. The warehouse had obviously received a direct hit. Some of the other walls still stood, but, with the exception of three shops at one end of the street, every building in it had been gutted. Lush weeds grew now out of the old cellar floors; notices said that it was forbidden to trespass among the ruins or to deposit rubbish.

Number 39 had been a garage set back from the street in a space behind two other buildings and approached by an arched drive-in between them. The arch was still standing. Fastened to its brickwork was a rusty metal sign. The words on it could be read: *"Garage und Reparaturwerkstatt. J. Schirmer—Bereifung, Zübehor, Benzin."*

They walked through the archway to the place where the garage had stood. The site had been cleared, but the plan of the building was still visible; it could not have been a very big garage. All that remained of it now was a repair pit. It was half full of rain water and there were pieces of an old packing case floating in it.

As they stood there, it began to rain again.

"We'd better see if we can find out anything from the shops at the end of the street," George said.

The proprietor of the second of the shops they tried was an electrical contractor, and he had some information. He had only been there three years himself and knew nothing of the Schirmers; but he did know something about the garage site. He had considered renting it for his own use. He had wanted to put up a workshop and storeroom there and use the rooms over his shop to live in. The ground had no street frontage and was therefore of little value. He had thought to get it cheaply; but the owner had wanted too much and so he had made other arrangements. The owner was a Frau Gresser, wife of a chemist in the laboratories of a big factory out at Leverkusen. When women started bargaining, you understand, it was best to . . . Yes, he had her address written down somewhere, though if the gentleman were considering the property, he personally would advise him to think twice before wasting his time arguing with . . .

Frau Gresser lived in an apartment on the top floor of a newly reconstructed building near the Barbarossa Platz. They had to call three times before they found her in.

She was a stout, frowzy, breathless woman in her late fifties. Her apartment was furnished in the cocktail-bar-functional style of prewar Germany, and crammed with Tyrolean knick-knacks. She listened suspiciously to their explanations of their presence there before inviting them to sit down. Then she went and telephoned her husband. After a while she came back and said that she was prepared to answer questions.

Ilse Schirmer, she said, had been her cousin and childhood friend.

"Are the Schirmers alive now?" George asked.

"Ilse Schirmer and her husband were killed in the big air attacks on the city in May 1942," Miss Kolin interpreted.

"Did Frau Gresser inherit the garage land from them?"

Frau Gresser showed signs of indignation when the question was put and spoke rapidly in reply.

"By no means. The land was hers—hers and her husband's, that is. Johann Schirmer's own business went bankrupt. She and her husband had set him up in business again for the sake of Ilse. Naturally, they had hoped also to make a profit, but it was goodness of heart that motivated them in the first place. The business, however, was theirs. Schirmer was only the manager. He had a percentage of the takings and an apartment over the garage. No one could say that he had not been generously treated. Yet, after so much had been done for him by his wife's friends, he had tried to cheat them over the takings."

78

"Who was his heir? Did he leave a will?"

"If he had had anything to leave except debts, his heir would have been his son, Franz."

"Did the Schirmers have any other children?"

"Fortunately, no."

"Fortunately?"

"It was hard enough for poor Ilse to feed and clothe one child. She was never strong, and with a husband like Schirmer, even a strong woman would have become ill."

"What was the matter with Schirmer?"

"He was lazy, he was dishonest, he drank. When poor Ilse married him she did not know. He deceived everyone. When we met him he had a prosperous business in Essen. We thought him clever. It was not until his father went away that the truth was known."

"The truth?"

"It was his father, Friedrich, who had the business head. He was a good accountant and he kept the son properly under control. Johann was only a mechanic, a workman with his hands. The father had the brains. He understood money."

"Did Friedrich own the business?"

"It was a partnership. Friedrich had lived and worked for many years in Switzerland. Johann was brought up there. He did not fight for Germany in the first war. Ilse met him in 1915 while she was staying with friends in Zurich. They married and remained in Switzerland to live. All their savings were in Swiss francs. In 1923, when the German mark failed, they all came back to Germany—Friedrich, Johann, Isle, and the child, Franz—and bought the garage in Essen cheap with their Swiss money. Old Friedrich understood business."

"Then Franz was born in Switzerland?"

"Winterthur is near Zurich, Mr. Carey," said Miss Kolin. "It was mentioned in the army papers, you remember. But he would still have to apply for Swiss nationality."

"Yes, I know all about that. Ask her why the partnership broke up."

79

Frau Gresser hesitated when she heard the question.

"As she has said, Johann had no head for——"

Frau Gresser hesitated again and was silent. Her plump face had become red and shiny with embarrassment. At last she spoke.

"She would prefer not to discuss the matter," said Miss Kolin.

"All right. Ask her about Franz Schirmer. Does she know what hapepned to him?"

He saw the relief in Frau Gresser's face when she understood that the subject of Friedrich Schirmer's departure was not going to be pursued. It made him curious.

"Franz was reported missing in Greece in 1944. The official letter addressed to his mother was forwarded to Frau Gresser."

"The report said: 'missing, believed killed.' Did she ever receive official confirmation of his death?"

"Not officially."

"What does she mean?"

"One of Franz's officers wrote to Frau Schirmer to tell her what had happened to her son. That letter also was forwarded to Frau Gresser. Having read it, she had no doubt that Franz was dead."

"Did she keep the letter? Is it possible for us to see it?"

Frau Gresser considered the request for a moment; finally she nodded and, going to a chest of drawers shaped as if to reduce its wind resistance, brought out a tin box full of papers. After a long search the officer's letter was found, together with the original army casualty notification. She handed both documents to Miss Kolin, making some explanation as she did so.

"Frau Gresser wishes to explain that Franz neglected to report to the army authorities that his parents had been killed and that it was the postal authorities who forwarded the letters."

"I see. What's the letter say?"

"It is from Lieutenant Hermann Leubner of the Engineer Company, Ninety-fourth Garrison Regiment. It is dated the 1st of December 1944,"

"What's the date that Franz was reported missing on that army notification?"

"October 31."

"All right."

"The Lieutenant writes: 'Dear Frau Schirmer: You will, no doubt, already have been notified by the army authorities of the fact that your son, Sergeant Franz Schirmer, has been listed as missing. I write as his officer to tell you of the circumstances in which this sad occurrence took place. It was on the 24th of October—'" She broke off.

"They were pulling out. They wouldn't trouble to send casualty returns every day," George said.

Miss Kolin nodded. "It continues: 'The regiment was moving westwards from Salonika towards the Greek frontier in the general direction of Florina. Sergeant Schirmer, as an experienced soldier and a responsible man, was sent with three trucks and ten men to a gasoline dump several kilometres off the main road near the town of Vodena. His orders were to load as much of the gasoline as he could onto the trucks, destroy the remainder, and return, bringing the troops who had been guarding the dump with him. Unfortunately, his detachment was ambushed by one of the Greek terrorist bands that had been attempting to hinder our operations. Your son was in the first truck, which exploded a mine laid by the terrorists. The third truck was able to stop in time to avoid most of the machine-gun fire of the terrorists, and two men from it were able to escape and rejoin the regiment. I myself led a force immediately to the place of the ambush. Your son was not among the dead we found and buried, nor was there any other trace of him. The driver of his truck was also missing. Your son was not a man to surrender unwounded. It is possible that he was rendered unconscious by the explosion of the mine and so captured. We do not know. But I would be failing in my duty if I encouraged you to hope that if he were captured by these Greeks he would be alive. They have not the military code of honour of us Germans. It is, of course, also possible that your son evaded capture but was unable to rejoin his comrades immediately. If so, you will be informed by the authorities when there is news of him. He was a brave man and a good soldier. If he is dead, then you will have the pride and consolation of knowing that he gave his life for his Führer and the Fatherland.' "

George sighed. "That all?"

"He adds: 'Heil Hitler,' and signs it."

"Ask Frau Gresser if she heard any more about it from the army authorities."

"No, she did not."

"Did she make any attempt to find out more? Did she try the Red Cross?"

"She was advised that the Red Cross could do nothing."

"When did she ask them?"

"Early in 1945."

"And not since?"

"No. She also asked the *Volksbund Deutsche Kriegsgräberfüsorge*—that is, the war-graves organization—for information. They had none."

"Was any application ever made to have him presumed dead?"

"There was no reason for such action."

"Does she know if he married?"

"No."

"Did she ever correspond with him?"

"She wrote a letter of sympathy to him when his parents were killed, but received no more than a bare acknowledgment from him. He did not even ask where they were buried. He showed a want of feeling, she thought. She sent a parcel soon afterwards. He did not trouble to write to thank her for it. She sent no more."

"Where did his reply come from in 1942?"

"From Benghazi."

"Did she keep the letter?"

"No."

Frau Gresser spoke again. George watched her plump face quivering and her small, resentful eyes flickering between her two visitors. He was getting used now to interpretation and had learned not to try to anticipate the conversation while he waited. He was thinking at the moment that it would be unpleasant to be under any sort of obligation to Frau Gresser. The rate of emotional interest she would charge would be exorbitantly high.

"She says," said Miss Kolin, "that she did not like Franz and had never liked him even as a child. He was a sullen, sulky boy and always ungrateful for kindness. She wrote to him only as a duty to his dead mother."

"How did he feel about foreigners? Had he any particular girl-friends? What I'm getting at is this—does she think he'd be the kind of man to marry a Greek girl, say, or an Italian, if he had the chance?"

Frau Gresser's reply was prompt and sour.

"She says that, where women were concerned, he was the sort of man who would do anything that his selfish nature suggested. He would do anything if he had the chance—except marry."

"I see. All right, I think that's about the lot. Would you ask her if we can borrow these papers for twenty-four hours to have photostats made?"

Frau Gresser considered the request carefully. Her small eyes became opaque. George could feel the documents suddenly becoming precious to her.

"I'll give her a receipt for them, of course, and they'll be returned tomorrow," he said. "Tell her the American Consul will have to notarize the copies or she could have them back today."

Frau Gresser handed them over reluctantly. While he was writing the receipt, George remembered something.

"Miss Kolin, have another try at finding out why Friedrich Schirmer left the business at Essen."

"Very well."

He lingered over the writing-out of the receipt. He heard Miss Kolin put the question. There was a momentary pause; then Frau Gresser replied with a positive volley of words. Here voice rose steadily in pitch as she spoke. Then she stopped. He signed the receipt and looked up to find her staring at him in a flustered, accusing sort of way. He handed her the receipt and put the documents in his pocket.

"She says," said Miss Kolin, "that the matter is not one which can be discussed in the presence of a man and that it can have no bearing on your inquiries. She adds, however, that if you do not believe that she is telling the truth, she will make the explanation confidentially to me. She will say no more on the subject while you are here."

"O.K. I'll wait for you downstairs." He rose and bowed to Frau Gresser. "Thank you very much indeed, madam. What you have told me is of inestimable help. I will see that your papers are safely returned to you tomorrow. Good day."

He smiled affably, bowed again, and went. He was outside the apartment almost before Miss Kolin had finished interpreting his farewell speech.

She joined him in the street below ten minutes later.

"Well," he said, "what was it all about?"

"Friedrich made advances to Ilse Schirmer."

"To his son's wife, you mean?"

"Yes."

"Well, well. Did she go into details?"

"Yes. She enjoys herself, that one."

"But the old man must have been around sixty then."

"You remember the photographs that Father Weichs destroyed?"

"Yes."

"He showed them to the wife."

"Just that?"

"His meaning apparently was unmistakable. He also proposed in a veiled way that he should take similar photographs of her."

"I see." George tried to picture the scene.

He saw a shabby room in Essen and an elderly bookkeeper sitting there pushing dog-eared photographs one by one across the table to where his son's wife could see them as she sat bent over her needlework.

How the man's heart must have beat as he watched

her face! His mind must have seethed with questions and doubts.

Would she smile or would she pretend to be shocked? She was sitting still, absolutely still, and she had stopped working. Soon she would smile, for certain. He could not see her eyes. After all, there was nothing wrong in a little private joke between a father and daughter-in-law, was there? She was a grown-up woman and knew a thing or two, didn't she? She liked him, he knew. All he wanted to do was show her that he wasn't too old for a bit of fun and that, even if Johann was no good, there was one man about the house for her to turn to. And now the last photograph, the sauciest of the lot. An eye-opener, eh? Good fun? She still hadn't smiled, but she hadn't frowned either. Women were funny creatures. You had to choose your moment; woo gently and then be bold. She was slowly raising her head now and looking at him. Her eyes were very round. He smiled and said what he had planned to say—that subtle remark about new pictures being better than old. But she did not smile back. She was getting to her feet and he could see that she was trembling. What what? Excitement? And then, suddenly, she had let out a sob of fear and run from the room out to the workshop where Johann was decarbonizing that Opel taxi. After that, everything had become a nightmare, with Johann shouting at and threatening him, and Ilse weeping, and the boy Franz standing there listening, white-faced, not understanding what it was all about; only knowing that in some way the world was coming to an end.

Yes, George thought, a pretty picture; though probably an inaccurate one. Still, it was the sort of scene about which nobody could ever be quite accurate; least of all, those who had taken part in it. He would never know what had really happened. Not that it mattered very much. Friedrich, Johann, and Ilse, the principal actors, were certainly dead. And Franz? He glanced at Miss Kolin marching along beside him.

"Do you think Franz is dead?" he asked.

85

"The evidence seemed conclusive. Did you not think so?"

"In a way, yes. If the man had been a friend of mine and had a wife and family he was fond of back home, I wouldn't try to kid his wife that he might still be alive. And if she were crazy enough to go on believing that he wasn't dead, I'd tell her as gently as I could to face the facts. But this is different. If we took the evidence we've got to court and asked for leave to presume Franz Schirmer dead, they'd laugh at us."

"I do not see why."

"Look. The man's in a truck ambushed by these guerrillas. That Lieutenant comes along some time afterwards and has a look at the scene. There are lots of dead bodies about, but not the dead body of our man. So maybe he's escaped and maybe he's a prisoner. If he's a prisoner, says the Lieutenant, then he hasn't a hope, because the Greek guerrillas had the habit of killing their prisoners. 'Just a minute,' says the judge; 'are you claiming that *all* Greek guerrillas operating in 1944 *invariably* killed *all* their prisoners? Are you prepared to prove that there were no cases at all of German soldiers surviving after capture?' What does the Lieutenant say to that? I don't know anything about the Greek campaign—I wasn't there—but I do know that if all these guerrillas were so well trained and so well organized and so trigger-happy that no German who fell into their hands was ever smart enough or lucky enough to get away, they'd have had the Germans pulling out of Greece long before the Normandy landings. All right, then, let's alter the wording of the evidence. Let's say that Greek guerrillas *often* killed their prisoners. Now, then—"

"But do you think he is *not* dead?" she asked.

"Of course I think he's dead. I'm just trying to point out there's a whole lot of difference between an ordinary everyday probability and the calculated kind that the law prefers. And the law's right. You'd be surprised how often people turn up when they've been thought dead. A man gets fired from his job and quarrels with his wife; so he goes down to the shore, takes off his coat, leaves it with a suicide note on the beach, and that's the last seen of him. Dead? Maybe. But sometimes he's found by accident years later living under a different name and with a different wife in a city on the other side of the continent."

She shrugged. "This is different."

"Not so very. Look at it this way. It's 1944. Let's suppose that Franz Schirmer is captured by the guerrillas but by luck or skill manages to get away alive. What is he to do? Rejoin his unit? The German occupation forces are trying to escape through Yugoslavia and having a tough time doing it. If he leaves his hideout and tries to catch up with them, he's certain to be recaptured by the guerrillas. They're all over the place now. It's better to stay where he is for a while. He is a resourceful man, trained to live off the country. He can stay alive. When it is safe for him to do so, he will go. Time passes. The country is under Greek control once again. Hundreds of miles now separate him from the nearest German unit. Civil war breaks out in Greece. In the resultant confusion he is able to make his way to the Turkish frontier and cross it without being caught. He is an engineer and does not mind work. He takes a job."

"By February 1945 Turkey was at war with Germany."

"Maybe it's before February."

"Then why does he not report to the German Consul?"

"Why should he? Germany is collapsing. The war is virtually over. Maybe he likes it where he is. Anyway, what has he to return to postwar Germany for? To see Frau Gresser? To see what's left of his parents' home? Maybe he married an Italian girl when he was in Italy and wants to get back there. He may even have children. There are dozens of possible reasons why he shouldn't go to the German Consul. Maybe he went to the Swiss one."

"If he had married, his army record would show it."

"Not if he married someone he wasn't supposed to

marry. Look at the rules the Americans and British had about their troops marrying German girls."

"What do you propose?"

"I don't know yet. I'll have to think."

When he got back to the hotel, he sat down and wrote a long cable to Mr. Sistrom. First he set out briefly the latest developments in the inquiry; then he asked for instructions. Should he return home now or should he go on and make an attempt to confirm Franz Schirmer's death?

The following afternoon he had the reply.

"HAVING LOOKED UNDER SO MANY STONES," it said, "SEEMS PITY LEAVE ONE UNTURNED STOP GO AHEAD TRY CONFIRM OR OTHERWISE FRANZ DEATH STOP SUGGEST GIVING IT THREE WEEKS STOP IF IN YOUR JUDGMENT NO SERIOUS HEADWAY MADE OR LIKELY BY THEN LETS FORGET IT. SISTROM."

That night George and Miss Kolin left Cologne for Geneva.

Miss Kolin had interpreted at conferences for the Internation Red Cross Committee and knew the people at headquarters who could be of help. George was soon put in touch with an official who had been in Greece for the Red Cross in 1944; a lean, mournful Swiss who looked as if nothing again could ever surprise him. He spoke good English and four other languages besides. His name was Hagen.

"There is no doubt at all, Mr. Carey," he said, "that the *andartes* did often kill their prisoners. I am not saying that they did it simply because they hated the enemy or because they had a taste for killing, you understand. It is difficult to see what else they could have done much of the time. A guerrilla band of thirty men or less is in no position to guard and feed the people it takes. Besides, Macedonia is in the Balkan tradition, and there the killing of an enemy can seem of small importance."

"But why take prisoners? Why not kill them at once?"

"Usually they were taken for questioning."

"If you were in my position, how would you go about establishing the death of this man?"

"Well, as you know where the ambush took place, you might try getting in touch with some of the *andartes* who were operating in that area. They might remember the incident. But I think I should say that you may find it difficult to persuade them to refresh their memories. Was it an ELAS band, do you know, or an EDES?"

"EDES?"

"The Greek initials stand for the National Democratic Liberation Army—the anti-Communist *andartes*. ELAS were the Communist *andartes*—the National Popular Liberation Army. In the Vodena area it would most likely be ELAS."

"Does it matter which it was?"

"It matters a great deal. There have been three years of civil war in Greece, you must remember. Now that the rebellion is over, those who fought on the Communist side are not easy to find. Some are dead, some in prison, some in hiding still. Many are refugees in Albania and Bulgaria. As things are, you would probably find it difficult to get in touch with ELAS men. It is complex."

"Yes, it sounds it. What real chance would there be, do you think, of my finding out what I want to know?"

Monsieur Hagen shrugged. "Often in such matters I have seen chance operate so strangely that I no longer try to estimate it. How important is your business, Mr. Carey?"

"There's a good deal of money at stake."

The other sighed. "So many things could have happened. You know, there were hundreds of men reported 'missing, believed killed' who had simply deserted. Salonika had plenty of German deserters towards the end of 1944."

"Plenty?"

"Oh, yes, of course. ELAS recruited most of them.

There were many Germans fighting for the Greek Communists around Christmas 1944."

"Do you mean to say that in late 1944 a German soldier could go about in Greece *without* getting killed?"

A pale smile drifted across Monsieur Hagen's mournful face. "In Salonika you could see German soldiers sitting in the cafés and walking about the streets."

"In uniform?"

"Yes, or part uniform. It was a curious situation. During the war the Communists in Yugoslavia, Greece, and Bulgaria had agreed to create a new Macedonian state. It was all part of a larger Russian plan for a Balkan Communist Federation. Well, the moment the Germans had gone, a force called the Macedonian Group of Divisions of ELAS took over Salonika and prepared to put the plan into execution. They didn't care any more about Germans. They had a new enemy to fight—the lawful Greek government. What they wanted to fight with were trained soldiers. It was Vafiades who had the idea of recruiting German deserters. He was the ELAS commander in Salonika then."

"Can't I get in touch with this Vafiades?" George asked.

He saw Miss Kolin stare at him. An expression of anxious perplexity came over Monsieur Hagen's face.

"I'm afraid that would be a little difficult, Mr. Carey."

"Why? Is he dead?"

"Well, there seems to be some doubt as to just what has happened to him." Monsieur Hagen seemed to be choosing his words. "The last we heard of him directly was in 1948. He then told a group of foreign journalists that, as head of the Provisional Democratic Government of Free Greece, he proposed to establish a capital on Greek soil. That was just about the time his army captured Karpenissi, I believe."

George looked blankly at Miss Kolin.

"Markos Vafiades called himself General Markos,"

she murmured. "He commanded the Greek Communist rebel army in the civil war."

"Oh, I see." George felt himself reddening. "I told you I didn't know anything about the Greek set-up," he said. "I'm afraid this kind of name-dropping misses with me."

Monsieur Hagen smiled. "Of course, Mr. Carey. We are closer to these things here. Valfiades was a Turkish-born Greek, a tobacco worker before the war. He was a Communist of many years' standing and had been to prison on that account. No doubt he had a respect for revolutionary tradition. When the Communists gave him command of the rebel army he decided to be known simply as Markos. It has only two syllables and is more dramatic. If the rebels had won he might have become as big a man as Tito. As it was, if you will forgive the comparison, he had something in common with your General Lee. He won his battles but lost the war. And for the same kind of reason. For Lee, the loss of Vicksburg and Atlanta, especially Atlanta, meant the destruction of his lines of communication. For Markos, also faced by superior numbers, the closing of the Yugoslav frontier had the same sort of effect. As long as the Communists of Yugoslavia, Bulgaria, and Albania helped him, he was in a strong position. By retiring across those frontiers, he was able to break off any action that looked like developing unfavourably. Then, behind the frontier, he could regroup and reorganize in safety, gather reinforcements, and appear again with deadly effect on a weakly held sector of the government front. When Tito quarrelled with Stalin and withdrew his support of the Macedonian plan, he cut Markos's lateral lines of communication in two. Greece owes much to Tito."

"But wouldn't Markos have been beaten in the end anyway?"

Monsieur Hagen made a doubtful face. "Maybe. British and American air did much. I do not dispute that. The Greek army and air force were completely transformed. But the denial of the Yugoslav frontier to Markos made it possible to use that power quickly and decisively. In January 1949, after over two years' fighting, the Markos forces were in possession of Naoussa, a big industrial town only eighty miles from Salonika itself. Nine months later they were beaten. All that was left was a pocket of resistance on Mount Grammos, near the Albanian frontier."

"I see." George smiled. "Well, there doesn't seem to be much likelihood of my being able to talk to General Vafiades, does there?"

"I'm afraid not, Mr. Carey."

"And even if I could, there wouldn't be much sense in my asking him about a German Sergeant who got caught in an ambush in '44."

Monsieur Hagen bowed his head politely. "None."

"So let me get it straight, sir. In 1944 the guerrillas —*andartes* you call them, do you?—the *andartes* killed some Germans and recruited others. Is that right?"

"Certainly."

"So that if the German soldier I'm interested in managed to get away alive after that ambush, it would not be fantastic to give him a fifty-fifty chance of staying alive?"

"Not at all fantastic. Very reasonable."

"I see. Thanks."

Two days later George and Miss Kolin were in Greece.

7

"FORTY-FIVE thousand killed, including three thousand five hundred civilians murdered by the rebels and seven hundred blown up by their mines. Twice as many wounded. Eleven thousand houses destroyed. Seven hundred thousand persons driven from their homes in rebel areas. Twenty-eight thousand forcibly removed to Communist countries. Seven thousand villages looted. That is what Markos and his friends cost Greece."

Colonel Chrysantos paused and, leaning back in his swivel chair, smiled bitterly at George and Miss Kolin. It was an effective pose. He was a very handsome man with keen, dark eyes. "And I have heard it said by the British and the Americans," he added, "that we have been too firm with our Communists. Too firm!" He threw up his long, thin hands.

George murmured vaguely. He knew that the Colonel's ideas of what constituted firmness were very different from his own and that a discussion of them would not be profitable. Monsieur Hagen, the Red Cross man, who had given him the letter of introduction to Colonel Chrysantos, had made the position clear. The Colonel was a desirable acquaintance only in so far as he was a senior officer in the Salonika branch of Greek military intelligence, who could lay his hands on the kind of information George needed. He was not a person towards whom it was possible to have very friendly feelings.

"Do these casualty figures include the rebels, Colonel?" he asked.

"Of the killed, yes. Twenty-eight of the forty-five thousand were rebels. About their wounded we have naturally no accurate figures; but in addition to those we killed, we captured thirteen thousand, and twenty-seven thousand more surrendered.

"Do you have lists of the names?"

"Certainly."

"Would it be possible to see if the name of this German is on one of those lists?"

"Of course. But you know we did not take more than a handful of Germans."

"Still it might be worth trying, though, as I say, I don't even know yet if the man survived the ambush."

"Ah, yes. Now we come to that. The 24th of October '44 was the date of the ambush, you say, and it was near a petrol point at Vodena. The *andartes*

93

might have come from the Florina area, I think. We shall see. So!"

He pressed a button on his desk and a young Lieutenant with horn-rimmed glasses came in. The Colonel spoke sharply in his own language for nearly half a minute. When he stopped, the Lieutenant uttered a monosyllable and went out.

As the door shut, the Colonel relaxed. "A good boy, that," he said. "You Westerners sometimes pride yourselves that we cannot be efficient, but you will see—like that!" He snapped his fingers, smiled seductively at Miss Kolin and then glanced at George to see if he minded having his girl smiled at in that way.

Miss Kolin merely raised her eyebrows. The Colonel passed round cigarettes.

George found the situation entertaining. The Colonel's curiosity about the nature of the relationship between his visitors had been evident from the first. The woman was attractive; the man looked passably virile; it was absurd to suppose that they could travel about together on business without also taking advantage of the association for their pleasure. Yet, of course, the man was an Anglo-Saxon and so one could not be sure. In the absence of any positive evidence as to whether the pair were lovers or not the Colonel was beginning to probe for some. He would try again in a moment or two. Meanwhile, back to business.

The Colonel smoothed his tunic down. "This German of yours, Mr. Carey—was he an Alsatian?"

"No, he came from Cologne."

"Many of the deserters were Alsatian. You know, some of them hated the Germans as much as we did."

"Ah, yes? Were you in Greece during the war, Colonel?"

"Sometimes. At the beginning, yes. Later I was with the British. In their raiding forces. It was a type of commando, you understand. That was a happy time."

"Happy?"

"Were you not a soldier, Mr. Carey?"

"I was a bomber pilot. I don't remember ever feeling particularly happy about it."

94

"Ah, no—but the air is different from soldiering. You do not see the enemy you kill. A machine war. Impersonal."

"It was personal enough for me," George said; but the remark went unheard. There was the light of reminiscence in the Colonel's eyes.

"You missed much in the air, Mr. Carey," he said dreamily. "I remember once, for example . . ."

He was off.

He had taken part, it seemed, in numerous British raids on German garrisons on Greek territory. He went on to describe in great detail what he obviously felt to be some of his more amusing experiences. Judging by the relish with which he recalled them, he had indeed had a happy time.

". . . splashed his brains over the wall with a burst from a Bren gun . . . put my knife low in his belly and ripped it open to the ribs . . . the grenades killed all of them in the room except one, so I dropped him out of the window . . . ran away without their trousers, so we could see what to shoot at . . . tried to come out of the house to surrender, but he was slow on his feet and the phosphorus grenade set him alight like a torch . . . I let him have a burst from the Schmeisser and nearly cut him in two . . ."

He spoke rapidly, smiling all the time and gesturing gracefully. Occasionally he broke into French. George made little attempt to follow. It did not matter, for the Colonel's whole attention now was concentrated on Miss Kolin. She was wearing her faintly patronizing smile, but there was something more in her expression besides—a look of pleasure. If you had been watching the pair of them without knowing what was being said, George thought, you might have supposed that the handsome Colonel was entertaining her with a witty piece of cocktail-party gossip. It was rather disconcerting.

The Lieutenant came back into the room with a tattered folder of papers under his arm. The Colonel stopped instantly and sat up straight in his chair to receive the folder. He looked through it sternly as the Lieutenant made his report. Once he rapped out a question and received an answer which appeared to satisfy him. Finally he nodded and the Lieutenant went out. The Colonel relaxed again and smirked complacently.

"It will take time to check the lists of prisoners," he said, "but, as I hoped, we have some other information. Whether it will be of help to you or not, I cannot say." He glanced down at the bundle of torn and greasy papers before him. "This ambush you mention was most likely one of several operations undertaken in that week by an ELAS band based in the hills above Florina. There were thirty-four men, most of them from Florina and the villages about there. The leader was a Communist named Phengaros. He came from Larisa. A German army truck was destroyed in the action. Does that sound like the case you know of?"

George nodded. "That's it. There were three trucks. The first hit a mine. Does it say anything about any prisoners?"

"Prisoners would not be reported, Mr. Carey. Fortunately, however, you can ask."

"Ask whom?"

"Phengaros." The Colonel grinned. "He was captured in '48. We have him under lock and key."

"Still?"

"Oh, he was released under an amnesty, but he is back now. He is a Party member, Mr. Carey, and a dangerous one. A brave man, perhaps, and a good one for killing Germans, but such politicals do not change their ways. You are lucky he has not long ago been shot."

"I was wondering why he wasn't."

"One could not shoot all of these rebels," the Colonel said with a shrug. "We are not Germans or Russkis. Besides, your friends in Geneva would not have liked it."

"Where can I see this man?"

"Here in Salonika. I shall have to speak to the commandant of the prison. Do you know your Consul here?"

"Not yet, but I have a letter to him from our Legation in Athens."

"Ah, good. I will tell the commandant that you are a friend of the American Minister. That should be sufficient."

"What exactly is this man Phengaros in prison for?"

The Colonel referred to the folder. "Jewel robbery, Mr. Carey."

"I thought you said he was a political prisoner."

"In America, Mr. Carey, your criminals are all capitalists. Here in these times they are occasionally Communists. Men like Phengaros do not steal for themselves, but for the Party funds. Of course, if we catch them they go to the criminal prison. They cannot be sent to the islands as politicals. They have made some big coups lately. It is quite traditional. Even the great Stalin robbed a bank for the Party funds when he was a young man. Of course, there are some of these bandits from the hills who only pretend to rob for the Party, and keep what they get for themselves. They are clever and dangerous and the police do not catch them. But Phengaros is not of that kind. He is a simple, deluded fanatic of the type that always gets caught."

"When can I see him?"

"Tomorrow perhaps. We shall see." He pressed the button again for the Lieutenant. "Tell me," he said, "are you and Madame by chance without an engagement this evening? I should so much like to show you our city."

Twenty minutes later George and Miss Kolin left the building and came again into the heat and glare of a Salonika afternoon. George's excuse that he had a long report to write that evening had been accepted with ready understanding. Miss Kolin had seemed to have rather more difficulty in evading the Colonel's hospitality. The conversation, however, had been conducted in Greek and George had understood nothing of it.

They crossed to the shade on the other side of the street.

"How did you manage to get out of it?" he asked as they turned towards the hotel.

"I explained that my stomach was upset by the food and the flies and that I should probably be sick all night."

George laughed.

"I spoke the truth."

"Oh, I'm sorry. Do you think you ought to see a doctor?"

"It will pass off. You have no stomach trouble yet?"

"No."

"It will come later. This is a bad place for the stomach when one is not used to it."

"Miss Kolin," George said after a while, "what did you really think of Colonel Chrysantos?"

"What can one think of such a man?"

"You didn't like him? He was very helpful and obliging."

"Yes, no doubt. It soothes his vanity to be helpful. There is only one thing that pleases me about that Colonel."

"Oh?"

She walked on several paces in silence. Then she spoke quietly, so quietly that he only just heard what she said.

"He knows how to deal with Germans, Mr. Carey."

It was at that moment that George received the first intimations of coming discomfort in his stomach and intestines. At that moment, also, he forgot about Colonel Chrysantos and Germans.

"I begin to see what you mean about the food and the flies," he remarked as they turned the corner by the hotel. "I think, if you don't mind, that we'll call in at a drugstore."

The following day the Colonel's Lieutenant arrived at their hotel in an army car and drove them out to the prison.

It was a converted barracks built near the remains of an old Turkish fort on the western outskirts of the city. With its high surrounding wall and the Kalamara Heights across the bay as a background, it looked from the outside rather like a monastery. Inside, it smelt like a large and inadequately tended latrine.

The Lieutenant had brought papers admitting them and they were taken to the administration block. Here they were introduced to a civilian official in a tight tussore suit, who apologized for the absence of the commandant on official business and offered coffee and cigarettes. He was a thin, anxious man, with a habit of picking his nose, of which he seemed to be trying, none too successfully, to break himself. When they had had their coffee, he took a heavy bunch of keys and led them through a series of passages with steel doors at both ends, which he unlocked and relocked as they went along. They were shown eventually into a room with whitewashed walls and a steel grille running down the middle from floor to ceiling. Through the grille they could see another door.

The official looked apologetic and mumbled something in bad French.

"Phengaros," Miss Kolin translated, "is not a good prisoner and sometimes behaves violently. The commandant would not wish us to be exposed to any trouble. It is for that reason that the interview must take place in these uncomfortable surroundings. He apologizes for them."

George nodded. He was not at ease. He had spent a disagreeable and exhausting night, and the smell of the place was making it difficult for him to forget the fact. Moreover, he had never been inside a prison before, and, while he had not supposed the experience would be anything but depressing, he had been unprepared for the lively sense of personal guilt that it aroused.

There was a sound from the door beyond the grille and he looked round. A Judas window had opened in it and a face was peering through. Then a key turned in the lock and the door opened. A man slowly entered the room.

The prisoner was thin and sinewy, with dark, sunken eyes and a long beak of a nose. His skin was brown and leathery as if he worked a lot in the sun. His shaven head had a black stubble of growth on it. He wore a cotton singlet and canvas trousers tied in at the waist with a strip of rag. His feet were bare.

He hesitated when he saw the faces on the other side of the grille, and the warder behind him prodded him with a club. He came forward into the light. The warder locked the door and stood with his back to it. The official nodded to George.

"Ask him what his name is," George said to Miss Kolin.

She relayed the question. The prisoner licked his lips, his dark eyes looking beyond her at the three men, as if she were the bait in a trap of their devising. He looked from her to the official and muttered something.

"What is the game?" Miss Kolin translated. "You know my name well enough. Who is this woman?"

The official shouted something at him violently and the warder prodded him again with the club.

George spoke quickly. "Miss Kolin, explain to him in as friendly a way as you can that I am an American lawyer and that my business has nothing to do with him personally. It is a private, legal matter. Say we only want to question him about that ambush at Vodena. There is no political angle to it. Our only object in questioning him is to confirm the death of a German soldier reported missing in 1944. Make it good."

As she spoke, George watched the prisoner's face. The dark eyes flickered suspiciously toward him as she went on. When she had finished, the prisoner thought for a moment. Then he answered.

"He will listen to the questions and decide whether he will answer when he has heard them."

Behind George the Lieutenant was beginning to mutter angrily to the official. George took no notice.

"O.K.," he said, "ask him his name. He's got to identify himself."

"Phengaros."

"Ask him if he remembers the ambush of the trucks."

"Yes, he remembers."

"He was in command of those particular *andartes?*"

"Yes."

"What happened exactly?"

"He does not know. He was not there."

"But he said—"

"He was leading an attack on the gasoline dump at the time. It was his second-in-command who caught the trucks."

"Where is his second-in-command?"

"Dead. He was shot a few months later by the fascist murder gangs in Athens."

"Oh. Well, ask him if he knows of any German prisoners taken from the trucks."

Phengaros thought for a moment, then nodded.

"Yes. One."

"Did he see this prisoner?"

"He interrogated him."

"What rank was he?"

"A private, he thinks. The man was the driver of the truck that hit the mine. He was wounded."

"Is he sure that there was no other prisoner?"

"Yes."

"Tell him we have information that there were two men in that first truck who did not return and whose bodies were not found by the German party that came on the scene later. One was the driver of the truck, whom he says he interrogated. The other was the Sergeant in charge of the detachment. We want to know what happened to the Sergeant."

Phengaros began gesturing emphatically as he talked.

"He says that he was not there, but that if there had been a German sergeant alive his men would certainly have taken him prisoner for questioning. A sergeant would have more information to give than a driver."

"What happened to the driver?"

"He died."

"How?"

There was a hesitation. "Of his wounds."

"O.K., we'll skip that. When he served in the army

101

of General Markos, did he come across any Germans fighting with it?"

"A few."

"Any whose name he can remember?"

"No."

"Ask him if he knows of anyone who actually took part in the truck ambush who's still alive."

"He knows of nobody."

"Surely they can't *all* be dead. Ask him to try and remember."

"He knows of nobody."

Phengaros was no longer looking at Miss Kolin now, but staring straight ahead.

There was a pause. George felt a touch on his arm. The Lieutenant drew him aside.

"Mr. Carey, this man does not wish to give information that might compromise his friends," he said in English.

"Oh, I see. Of course."

"Excuse me a moment, please."

The Lieutenant went to the official and held a whispered conversation with him. Then he returned to George.

"The information might be obtained for you, Mr. Carey," he murmured, "but it would take time to do so."

"How do you mean?"

"This Phengaros is a difficult man to persuade, it seems, but, if you wish, some disciplinary pressure might be applied—"

"No, no." George spoke hastily; his knees were beginning to tremble. "Unless he gives the information quite voluntarily it can have no legal value as evidence." It was a dishonest excuse. Phengaros's evidence had no legal value anyway; it was the evidence of eye-witnesses (if any) that would be important. But George could think of nothing better.

"As you please. Is there anything else you wish to ask?" The Lieutenant's manner was bored now. He had seen through George. If the inquiry could be pursued with such lily-livered timidity, it could not be of very great importance.

"I don't think so, thanks." George turned to Miss Kolin. "Ask this prison man if it's against the rules to give the prisoner some cigarettes."

The official stopped picking his nose when he heard the question. Then he shrugged. If the American wished to waste cigarettes on such an un-co-operative type he might do so; but they must be examined first.

George took out a packet of cigarettes and handed it to him. The official glanced inside, pinched the packet, and handed it back. George held it through the grille.

Phengaros had been standing there with a faint smile on his face. His eyes met George's. With an ironic bow he took the cigarettes. As he did so he began to speak.

"I understand the feelings of embarrassment that prompt you to offer this gift," translated Miss Kolin. "If I were a criminal, I would gladly accept them. But the fate of my comrades at the hands of the fascist reactionaries already rests too lightly on the conscience of the world. If your own conscience is troubling you, sir, that is to your credit. But I am not yet so corrupted here as to allow you to ease it for the price of a packet of cigarettes. No. Much as I should have enjoyed smoking them, sir, I think that their destination must be that of all other American aid."

With a flick of his wrist he tossed the cigarettes to the warder behind him.

They fell on the floor. As the warder snatched them up, the official began shouting to him angrily through the grille and he hastened to unlock the door.

Phengaros nodded curtly and went out.

The official stopped shouting and turned apologetically to George. *"Une espèce de fausse-couche,"* he said; *"je vous demande pardon, monsieur."*

"What for?" said George. "If he thinks I'm a lousy crypto-fascist-imperialist lackey, he's quite right in refusing to smoke my cigarettes."

"Pardon?"

"He also had the good manners not to heave the cigarettes right back in my face. In his place, I might have done just that."

"Qu'est ce que Monsieur a dit?"

The official was looking desperately at Miss Kolin.

George shook his head. "Don't bother to translate, Miss Kolin. He won't get it. You understand me, though, don't you, Lieutenant? Yes, I thought so. Now, if you don't mind, I'd like to get the hell out of here before something very inconvenient happens inside my stomach."

When they got back to the hotel, there was a note from Colonel Chrysantos awaiting them. It contained the information that a search of all the relevant lists had failed to discover anybody named Schirmer who had been either killed or captured in the Markos campaign; nor had an amnesty been granted to anyone of that name.

"Miss Kolin," George said, "what can you drink when you have this stomach thing?"

"Cognac is best."

"Then we'd better have some."

Later, when the experiment had been tried, he said: "When we were in Cologne my office gave me permission to go on with the investigation for three more weeks if I thought we were making progress. One of them's gone, and all we've found out is that Franz Schirmer most likely didn't get taken prisoner by the people who shot up the trucks."

"Surely, that is something."

"It's mildly interesting at best. It doesn't get us anywhere. I'm giving it one more week. If we're no nearer the truth by then, we go home. O.K.?"

"Perfectly. What will you do with the week?"

"Do what I have an idea I should have done before. Go to Vodena and look for his grave."

VODENA, WHICH used to be called Edessa and was once the seat of the kings of Macedon, is some fifty miles west of Salonika. It hangs, amid lush growth of vine and wild pomegranate, fig, and mulberry trees, in the foothills of Mount Chakirka six hundred feet above the Yiannitsa plain. Sparkling mountain streams cascade lyrically down the hillsides into Nisia Voda, the tributary of the Vadar which flows swiftly past the town on its way to the parent river. The old tiled houses glow in the sun. There are no tourist hotels.

George and Miss Kolin were driven there in a car hired in Salonika. It was not an enjoyable trip. The day was hot and the road bad. The condition of their stomachs denied them even the consolations of a good lunch and a bottle of wine at their destination. While the chauffeur went off heartily in search of food and wine, they went into a café, fought the flies for long enough to drink some brandy, and then dragged themselves off dispiritedly in search of information.

Almost immediately luck was with them. A sweetmeat pedlar in the market not only remembered the ambush well, but had actually been working in a near-by vineyard at the time. He had been warned to keep clear by the *andartes,* who had arrived an hour before the German trucks came.

When the chauffeur returned they persuaded the pedlar to leave his tray of flyblown titbits with a friend and guide them to the scene.

The fuel dump had been near a railway siding about three miles out of Vodena, on the side road to Apsalos.

The trucks had been caught about two miles along this stretch of road.

It was an ideal place for an ambush. The road was climbing steadily and at that point made a hairpin turn below a hillside with plenty of cover for the attackers among its trees and thickets. Below and beyond the road there was no cover at all. The mines had been placed well past the turn so that, when the first truck hit, it would block the road for those following at a point where they could neither turn their vehicles nor find cover from which to reply to the fire from above. For the *andartes* concealed on the hillside the business must have been easy. The remarkable thing was that as many as two of the eleven Germans in the trucks had managed to get back down the road alive. They must have been exceptionally nimble or the fire from the hillside very wild.

Those who had died had been buried lower down the hill in a patch of level ground just off the road. According to the pedlar, the ground had been damp with rain at the time. The neat row of graves was still discernible in the undergrowth. Lieutenant Leubner and his men had piled stones in a small cairn on each. George had seen wayside German graves in France and Italy and guessed that originally each grave had also borne its occupant's steel helmet, and perhaps a wooden stake with his number, name, and rank. It depended on how much time there had been to spare for such refinements. He looked for the stakes, but if they had ever existed, there was now no sign of them. Under a near-by bush he found a rusty German helmet; that was all.

"Seven graves," remarked Miss Kolin as they walked up the hill again; "that is what one would expect from the Lieutenant's letter to Frau Schirmer. Ten men and the Sergeant went. Two men return. The bodies of the Sergeant and the driver of the first truck are missing. Seven are buried."

"Yes, but Phengaros said that there was only one prisoner—the driver. So where was the Sergeant? Look! The driver was wounded when the truck hit the

106

mine, but not killed. Most likely the Sergeant was in the cab beside him. Probably he was wounded too. Lieutenant Leubner said he wasn't a man to surrender without a fight. Supposing he managed somehow to get clear of the road and was hunted down and killed some distance from it."

"But how, Mr. Carey? How could he get clear?"

They had reached the place of the ambush again. George walked along the edge of the road away from the hillside and looked down.

The bare rocky ground fell away precipitously to the valley below. It was absurd to suppose that even an unwounded man would attempt to scramble down it under fire from the hillside and the road above. The two men who had escaped had been able to do so because they were in the last truck and unwounded. The Sergeant had been a full two hundred yards farther away from cover. He had had no chance at all of getting clear.

George climbed a short way up the hillside to look at the scene from the attackers' point of view. From there, the plight of the men in the trucks seemed even more hopeless. He could imagine the scene: the trucks grinding up the hill, the ear-splitting detonation of the mine, the rattle of machine-gun and rifle fire, the thudding explosions of grenades lobbed on to the road, the hoarse shouts, the screams of the dying.

He clambered down to the car again.

"All right, Miss Kolin," he said; "what do *you* think happened?"

"I think that he was taken prisoner with the driver and that both were wounded. I think that the Sergeant died of his wounds or was killed trying to escape on the way to the *andartes'* rendezvous with Phengaros. Naturally Phengaros would think that only one prisoner had been taken."

"What about the Sergeant's papers? They would have been taken to Phengaros."

"They would also take the papers of those they had killed here."

George considered. "Yes, you may be right. At least

107

it's a reasonable explanation. There's still only one way we can find out for certain though, and that's by getting hold of someone who was there."

Miss Kolin nodded towards the pedlar. "I have been talking to this man. He says that the *andartes* who did this were from Florina. That agrees with the Colonel's information."

"Did he know any of them by name?"

"No. They just said they were from Florina."

"Another dead end. All right, we'll go there tomorrow. We'd better start back now. How much money do you think I should give this old man?"

It was early evening when they arrived back in Salonika. Something unusual seemed to have happened while they had been away. There were extra police on duty in the streets and shopkeepers stood in the roadway conferring volubly with their neighbors. The cafés were crowded.

At the hotel they heard the news.

Just before three o'clock that afternoon a closed army truck had driven up to the entrance of the Eurasian Credit Bank in the rue Egnatie. It had waited there for a moment or so. Then, suddenly, the covers at the back had been flung open and six men had jumped out. They had been armed with machine-pistols and grenades. Three of them had immediately stationed themselves in the entrance portico. The other three had gone inside. Within little more than two minutes they had been out again with several hundred thousand dollars' worth of foreign currency in American dollars, escudos, and Swiss francs. Ten seconds later, and almost before the passers-by had noticed that anything was wrong, they had been back in the truck and away.

The affair had been perfectly organized. The raiders had known exactly which safe the money was kept in and exactly how to get to it. No one had been shot. A clerk, who had courageously tried to set off an alarm bell, had received no more than a blow in the face from a gun butt for his audacity. The alarm bell had not sounded for the simple reason, discovered later, that the wires to it had been disconnected. The raiders had saluted with the clenched fist. Quite clearly they had had a Communist confederate inside the bank. Quite clearly the robbery was yet another in a series organized to replenish the Communist Party funds. Quite naturally suspicion as to the identity of the confederate had fallen upon the courageous clerk. Would he have dared to do what he did unless he had known in advance that he was running no risk? Of course not! The police were questioning him.

That was the receptionist's excited account of the affair.

The hotel barman confirmed the facts but had a more sophisticated theory about the motives of the criminals.

How was it, he asked, that every big robbery that now took place was the work of Communists stealing for the Party funds? Did nobody else steal any more? Oh yes, no doubt there *had* been political robberies, but not as many as people supposed. And why should the brigands give the clenched fist salute as they left? To show that they were Communists? Absurd! They were merely seeking to give that impression in order to deceive the police by directing attention away from themselves. They could count on the police preferring to blame Communists. Everything bad was blamed on the Communists. He himself was not a Communist of course, but . . .

He went on at length.

George listened absently. At that moment he was more interested in the discovery that his appetite had suddenly begun to return and that he could contemplate without revulsion the prospect of dinner.

Florina lies at the entrance to a deep valley nine miles south of the Yugoslav frontier. About forty miles away across the mountains to the west is Albania. Florina is the administrative centre of the province which bears its name and is an important railhead. It has a garrison and a ruined Turkish citadel. It has more than one hotel. It is neither as picturesque as Vodena nor as ancient. It came into existence as an insignificant staging point on a Roman road from Durazzo to Constantinople, and far too late to share in the short-lived glories of the Macedonian Empire. In a land which has contained so many of the springs of Western civilization, it is a parvenu.

But if Florina has no history of much interest to the compilers of guidebooks, it has, in the Edwardian sense of the word, a Past.

In the summer of 1896, sixteen men attended a meeting in Salonika. There they founded a political organization which in later years was to become the most formidable secret terrorist society the Balkans, or for that matter Europe, has known. It was called the Internal Macedonian Revolutionary Organization; IMRO, for short. Its creed was "Macedonia for the Macedonians," its flag a red skull and crossbones on a black ground, its motto "Freedom or Death." Its arguments were the knife, the rifle, and the bomb. Its armed forces, who lived in the hills and mountains of Macedonia enforcing IMRO laws and imposing IMRO taxes on the villagers and townspeople, were called *comitadjis*. Their oath of allegiance was sworn upon a Bible and a revolver, and the penalty for disloyalty was death. Among those who took this oath and served IMRO there were rich men as well as peasants, poets as well as soldiers, philosophers as well as professional murderers. In the cause of Macedonian autonomy it killed Turks and Bulgars, Serbs and Vlachs, Greeks and Albanians. It also killed Macedonians in the same cause. By the time of the First Balkan War, IMRO was a serious political force, capable of bringing considerable influence to bear upon events. The Macedonian *comitadji* with his cartridge belts and his rifle was becoming a legendary figure, a heroic defender of women and children against the savagery of the Turks, a knight of the mountains who preferred death to dishonour and treated his captives with courtesy and forbearance. The facts, harped upon by cynical observers, that the savageries of the Turks were gen-

110

erally committed by way of reprisal for atrocities committed by the *comitadjis*, and that the chivalrous behaviour was only in evidence when there was a chance of its impressing foreign sympathizers, seemed to have little effect on the legend. It persisted remarkably and has to some extent continued to do so. In the main square of Gorna Djoumaia, the capital of Bulgarian Macedonia, there is even a monument to "The Unknown *Comitadji*." True, it was put up in 1933 by the IMRO gangsters who ran the city; but the Bulgarian central government of the time did not object to it, and it is almost certainly still there. If IMRO is no longer served by poets and idealists, it remains a political force and has from time to time sold itself with nice impartiality to both Fascists and Communists. IMRO is and always has been a very Balkan institution.

Florina was one of the "founder" strongholds of IMRO. Soon after the momentous Salonika meeting in 1896, an ex-Sergeant of the Bulgarian army named Marko began recruiting an IMRO band in Florina, which rapidly became the most powerful in the area. And the most distinguished. The Bulgarian poet Yavorov and the young writer Christo Silianov were among those who chose to join it, and (though Silianov, the writer, disgraced himself by showing an effeminate aversion to cutting his prisoners' throats) both saw much active service with the Florina men. Marko himself was killed by Turkish soldiers, but the band remained an effective unit and played a prominent part in the rebellion of 1903. The irredentist techniques of sabotage, ambush, kidnapping, intimidation, armed robbery, and murder are part of Florina's cultural heritage; and although it now takes invasion and a war to induce the law-abiding inhabitants of the province to turn to these old skills, there are always, even in times of peace, a few daring spirits ready to take to the mountains and remind their unfortunate neighbours that the traditions of their forefathers are still very much alive.

111

George and Miss Kolin arrived by train from Salonika.

The Parthenon Hotel was a three-story building near the centre of the town. There was a café beneath it, and a restaurant which could be entered directly from the street. It was about the size of a third-class commercial hotel in a town like Lyon. The rooms were small and the plumbing primitive. The bedstead in George's room was of iron, but there was a wooden frame round the springs. At Miss Kolin's suggestion, George spent his first half-hour there with an insufflator and a canister of D.D.T., spraying the crevices in the woodwork. Then he went down to the café. Presently Miss Kolin joined him.

The proprietor of the Parthenon was a small, grey-faced man with grey hair cut *en brosse* and a crumpled grey suit. When he saw Miss Kolin appear, he left a table by the bar counter, at which he had been standing talking to an army officer, and came over to them. He bowed and said something in French.

"Ask him if he'll join us for a drink," George said.

When the invitation had been interpreted, the little man bowed again, sat down with a word of apology, and snapped his fingers at the barman.

They all had *oyzo*. Politenesses were exchanged. The proprietor apologized for not speaking English and then began discreetly to pump them about their business in the town.

"We have few tourists here," he remarked; "I have often said that it is a pity."

"The scenery is certainly very fine."

"If you have time while you are here you should take a drive. I shall be happy to arrange a car for you."

"Very kind of him. Say that we heard in Salonika that there was excellent hunting to be had near the lakes to the west."

"The gentleman is intending to go hunting?"

"Not this time, unfortunately. We are on business. But we were told that there was plenty of game up there."

The little man smiled. "There is game of all sorts in the neighbourhood. There are also eagles in the hills," he added slyly.

"Eagles who do a little hunting themselves, perhaps?"

"The gentleman learned that in Salonika, too, no doubt."

"I have always understood that this is a most romantic part of the country."

"Yes, the eagle is a bird of romance to some," the proprietor said archly. Obviously, he was the kind of person who could not let the smallest joke go, once he had got his teeth into it.

"It's a bird of prey, too."

"Ah, yes indeed! When armies disintegrate, there are always a few who prefer to stay together and fight a private war against society. But here in Florina the gentleman need have no fear. The eagles are safe in the hills."

"That's a pity. We were hoping you might be able to help us to find one."

"To find an eagle? The gentleman deals in fine feathers?"

But George was getting bored. "All right," he said, "we'll cut the double-talk. Tell him I'm a lawyer and that we want, if possible, to talk to someone who was in the ELAS band led by Phengaros in 1944. Explain that it's nothing political, that we just want to check up on the grave of a German Sergeant who was killed near Vodena. Say I'm acting for the man's relatives in America."

He watched the little man's face as Miss Kolin translated. For a moment or two a quite extraordinary expression came over its loose grey folds, an expression compounded of equal parts of interest, amazement, indignation, and fear. Then a curtain came down and the face went blank. Its owner picked up his drink and drained the glass.

"I regret," he said precisely, "that that is not a matter in which I can be of any assistance to you at all."

113

He rose to his feet.

"Wait a minute," said George. "If he can't help me, ask him if he knows of anyone here who can."

The proprietor hesitated, then glanced across at the officer sitting at the table by the bar. "One moment," he said curtly. He went over to the officer, and bending over the table, began talking in a rapid undertone.

After a moment or two, George saw the officer look across quickly at him, then say something sharply to the proprietor. The little man shrugged. The officer stood up and came over to them.

He was a lean, dark young man with lustrous eyes, very wide riding-breeches, and a waist like a girl's. He wore the badges of a captain. He bowed to Miss Kolin and smiled pleasantly at George.

"I beg your pardon, sir," he said in English. "The patron tells me that you are here making inquiries."

"That's right."

He clicked his heels. "Streftaris, Captain," he said. "You are an American, Mr——?"

"Carey's my name. Yes, I'm an American."

"And this lady?"

"Miss Kolin is French. She is my interpreter."

"Thank you. Perhaps I can be of assistance to you, Mr. Carey."

"That's very kind of you, Captain. Sit down, won't you?"

"Thank you." The Captain spun the chair round, swung the seat between his legs, and sat down with his elbows resting on the back. There was something curiously insolent about the gesture. He smiled less pleasantly. "You have made the patron feel very uneasy, Mr. Carey."

"I'm sorry about that. All I asked him was to put me in touch with someone who was in the Phengaros band in 1944. I told him there was nothing political about my business."

The Captain sighed elaborately. "Mr. Carey," he said, "if I were to come to you in America and ask you to put me in touch with a gangster wanted by the police, would you be prepared to help me?"

"Is that a true comparison?"

"Certainly. I do not think you quite understand our problems here. You are a foreigner, of course, and that excuses you, but it is very indiscreet to inquire into matters of this kind."

"Do you mind telling me why?"

"These men are Communists—outlaws. Do you know that Phengaros himself is in prison on a criminal charge?"

"Yes. I interviewed him two days ago."

"Pardon?"

"Colonel Chrysantos in Salonika was kind enough to arrange for me to see Phengaros in prison."

The Captain's smile faded. He took his elbows off the back of the chair.

"I beg your pardon, Mr. Carey."

"What for?"

"I did not understand that you were on official business."

"Well, to be exact—"

"I do not think we have received orders from Salonika. Had we done so, of course, the Commandant would have instructed me."

"Now, just a moment, Captain, let's get this straight. My business is legal rather than official. I'll explain."

The Captain listened carefully to the explanation. When George had finished he looked relieved.

"Then it is not on the advice of Colonel Chrysantos that you are here, sir?"

"No."

"You must know, Mr. Carey, that I am military intelligence officer for the district. It would be most unfortunate for me if Colonel Chrysantos thought—"

"Sure, I know. A very efficient man, the Colonel."

"Ah, yes."

"And a busy one. So, you see, I thought it might be better if I didn't trouble the Colonel again, but just got the names of some of these people unofficially."

The Captain looked puzzled. "Unofficially? How un-officially?"

"I could buy the names, couldn't I?"

"But from whom?"

"Well, that was what I was hoping the patron might be able to tell me."

"Ah!" The Captain at last permitted himself to smile again. "Mr. Carey, if the patron knew where the names that you want could be bought, he would not be so foolish as to admit the fact to a stranger."

"But haven't you a line on *any* of these people? What happened to them all?"

"Some were killed with the Markos forces, some are across the border with our neighbours. The rest" —he shrugged—"they have taken other names."

"But they're somewhere about here, surely."

"Yes, but I cannot recommend you to go looking for them. There are cafés in this town where, if you asked the questions you asked the patron here tonight, there would be much unpleasantness for you."

"I see. What would you do in my place, Captain?"

The Captain thought carefully for a moment, then he leaned forward. "Mr. Carey, I would not wish you to believe that I am not anxious to give you all the assistance I can."

"No, of course not."

But the Captain had not finished. "I wish to help you all I can. Please, however, explain to me one thing. You wish simply to know if this German Sergeant was killed or not killed in the ambush. Is that right?"

"That's right."

"You do not specially wish to know the name of the person who saw him die?"

George considered. "Well, let's put it this way," he said finally; "the probability is that the Sergeant *did* die. If he did and I can be reasonably certain of the fact, then that's all I want to know. My business is finished."

The Captain nodded. "Ah. Now let us suppose for a moment that such information could be obtained in some way. Would you be prepared to pay perhaps three hundred dollars for that information without knowing where it came from?"

116

"Three hundred! That's rather a lot isn't it?"

The Captain waved the subject away deprecatingly. "Let us say two hundred. The sum is not important."

"Then let's say one hundred."

"As you will. But would you pay, Mr. Carey?"

"Under certain conditions, yes."

"What conditions, please?"

"Well, I can tell you right now that I'm not going to pay out a hundred dollars just for the pleasure of having someone tell me that he knows somebody else who knows a man who was in that ambush and says that the German Sergeant was killed. I'd want some kind of evidence that the story was genuine."

"I understand that, but what evidence could there be?"

"Well, for one thing, what I'd want is a reasonable explanation of the fact that the Sergeant's body was not found by the German patrol that came along afterwards. There were dead men there, but the Sergeant wasn't among them. A genuine witness ought to know the answer to that one."

"Yes, that is logical."

"But is there any chance of getting the information?"

"That is what I have been thinking about. I see a chance, perhaps, yes. I can promise nothing. Do you know anything of police methods?"

"Only the usual things."

"Then you will know that when one is dealing with criminals, it is sometimes wise to give the less dangerous ones temporary immunity, and even encouragement, if by doing so one can know a little of what is going on among the rest."

"You mean paid informers?"

"Not quite. The paid informer is rarely satisfactory. One pays and pays for nothing and then, when he is about to be useful, he is found with his throat cut and the government's money is wasted. No, the types I am discussing are the lesser criminals whose activities can be tolerated because they know and are trusted by those whom we may wish to put our hands on. Such types will not inform, you understand, but by seeming

117

to be friendly and ready to overlook their little games one can learn much of what goes on that is interesting."

"I understand. If there were money in it and nobody risked incriminating himself, such a person might find out what I wanted to know."

"Exactly."

"Have you someone in mind?"

"Yes, but I must make a discreet inquiry first to see if an approach can safely be made. I think that Colonel Chrysantos would be very annoyed with me, Mr. Carey, if I put your life in danger"—he flashed a lustrous smile at Miss Kolin—"or that of Madame."

Miss Kolin looked down her nose.

George grinned. "No, we mustn't annoy the Colonel. But all the same it's very kind of you to take all this trouble, Captain."

The Captain raised a protesting hand. "It is nothing. If you should hapepn to mention to the Colonel that I was of some small assistance to you, I should be well repaid."

"Naturally I shall mention it. But who is this person you think might fix it up?"

"It is a woman. Outwardly she is the proprietress of a wineshop. In fact she deals secretly in arms. If a man wishes a rifle or a revolver, he goes to her. She gets it for him. Why do we not arrest her? Because then someone else would begin to deal, someone we might not know and could not so easily keep under surveillance. One day, perhaps, when we can be sure of stopping her sources of supply, we will take her. Until then, things are better as they are. She has a love of gossip and for your purpose is most suitable."

"But doesn't she know she's under surveillance?"

"Ah, yes, but she bribes my men. The fact that they take her money makes her feel safe. It is all quite friendly. But we do not wish to alarm her, so she must be consulted first." He rose to his feet, suddenly businesslike. "Perhaps tonight."

"That's good of you, Captain. Won't you stay and have a drink?"

"Ah, no, thank you. Just now I have various appointments. Tomorrow I will send a note to you here to give you the address to go to if she has agreed, and any other necessary instructions."

"O.K. Fine."

There was a lot of heel-clicking and politeness and he went. George signaled to the barman.

"Well, Miss Kolin," he said when they were served again, "what do you think?"

"I think that the Captain's various appointments are almost certainly with his mistress."

"I meant do you think there's anything in this. You know this part of the world. Do you think he'll do what he said about contacting this woman?"

She shrugged. "I think that for a hundred dollars the Captain would do almost anything."

It took a moment or two for George to appreciate the implication of this statement. "But the Captain's not getting the money," he said.

"No?"

"No. That's for the wineshop woman, if she comes through with the information."

"I do not think he will give her a hundred dollars. Perhaps twenty. Perhaps nothing."

"You're kidding."

"You asked me for my impression."

"He's the Keen Young Executive type. All he wants is a pat on the back from the boss. You see."

Miss Kolin smiled sardonically.

George did not get much rest that night. The precautions he had taken against bedbugs had somehow served to convince him that the mattress frame must be alive with the creatures. In the darkness he had soon begun to imagine that he was being attacked by them. Useless now to remind himself of the D.D.T. he had applied; Balkan bugs probably ate the stuff like ice cream. After a fourth panic inspection failed to reveal even one attacker, he became desperate, stripped the bed, and made a further assault on the mattress with the insufflator. A rose-coloured dawn was glowing among the mountain peaks before he succeeded in going to sleep.

He awoke, resentfully, at nine o'clock. While he was at breakfast in the café downstairs, a letter arrived from the Captain.

DEAR SIR [George read]:
The woman is Madame Vassiotis at the wineshop in the rue Monténégrine. She will expect you, but not until this afternoon. Say that you come from Monsieur Kliris. Do not refer to me. She has been told what you want and might have an answer for you. The price will be U. S. dollars 150, but do not give it to the woman herself or speak of it. I wish to be assured personally that you are satisfied before you pay. If, when I have seen you this evening, you tell me that all is well, I will see that the money goes to her by Monsieur Kliris.

The letter was written on plain paper and unsigned. George did not show it to Miss Kolin.

The rue Monténégrine proved to be a steep, refuse-strewn lane in the poorer quarter of the town. The houses were broken down and ugly. Lines of dingy washing were strung across the lane between some of the upper windows; others had bedding hung out over the sills. There were a great many children about.

The wineshop was near the top of the lane by a builder's yard. It had no display window. There was a bead-curtained doorway in a wall, and two or three steps led down to the interior. George and Miss Kolin entered and found themselves in a kind of cellar, with wine barrels stacked on their sides against the walls, and a massive wooden bench in the center. Light came from an oil lamp on a shelf. The air was cool and there was a smell of stale wine and old barrels that was not unpleasant.

There were two persons in the shop. One of them, an old man in the blue denim trousers, sat on the bench drinking a glass of wine. The other was Madame Vassiotis.

She was amazingly fat, with huge pendulous breasts

120

and a vast lap. She was sitting on, and almost completely enveloping, a low stool by a doorway at the back of the shop. When they entered, she rose slowly to her feet and waddled forward into the light.

Her head was small for her body, with dark hair drawn tightly away from the brow. The face seemed as though it ought to belong to someone younger or less gross. It was still firm and delicately shaped, and the eyes under their heavy lids were dark and clear.

She murmured a word of greeting.

Miss Kolin replied. George had briefed her in readiness for the interview and she did not trouble to interpret the preliminaries. He saw Madame Vassiotis nod understandingly and glance at the old man. He promptly finished his wine and went out. Then she bowed slightly to George and, with a gesture of invitation, led the way through a doorway at the back into a sitting-room.

There, there were Turkish carpets on the walls, a divan with plush cushions, and a few pieces of rickety Victorian furniture. It reminded him of a fortune-teller's booth in a travelling fair. Only the crystal ball was missing.

Madame Vassiotis poured three glasses of wine, sank down heavily on the divan, and motioned them to chairs. When they were seated, she folded her hands in her lap and looked placidly from one to the other of them as if waiting for someone to propose a parlour game.

"Ask her," George said, "if she has been able to get any reply to the questions put to her by Monsieur Kliris."

Madame Vassiotis listened gravely to the translation and then, with a nod, began to speak.

"She states," said Miss Kolin, "that she has been able to speak with one of the *andartes* who took part in the affair near Vodena. Her information is that the German Sergeant was killed."

"Does she know how he was killed?"

"He was in the first truck of the German convoy. It exploded a mine."

George thought for a moment. He had not mentioned either of those facts to the Captain. It was promising.

"Did the informant see the Sergeant dead?"

"Yes."

"Was he on the road?"

"He was where he fell when the truck was hit."

"What happened to the body afterwards?"

He saw Madame Vassiotis shrug.

"Does she know that the body was not there when the German patrol came along afterwards?"

"Yes, but her informant can offer no explanation of this."

George thought again. This was awkward. An experienced man would probably know that the N.C.O. in charge of a German column would ride in the leading truck; and certainly anyone who had taken any part at all in the ambush would know that the leading truck had hit a mine. The informant might well have been farther down the road, firing on the other trucks. With the prospect of earning a few dollars for his trouble, however, he would be ready to oblige with a reasonable guess.

"Ask her if her friend knows what the Sergeant's injuries were."

"She cannot say exactly. The Sergeant was lying in a pool of blood."

"Is she absolutely sure in her own mind—?" Then he broke off. "No, wait a minute. Put it another way. If the Sergeant were her own son, would she be satisfied in her own mind that he was dead from what her friend has told her?"

A smile appeared on the delicately curved lips and a chuckle shook the massive body as their owner understood his question. Then, with a grunting effort, she heaved herself up from the divan and waddled to a drawer in the table. From it she took a slip of paper, which she handed to Miss Kolin with an explanation.

"Madame anticipated your doubts and asked for proof that her friend saw the body. He told her that they stripped the dead Germans of their equipment and that he got the Sergeant's water bottle. He still has it. It has the Sergeant's number and name burned into the strap. They are written on this paper."

Madame Vassiotis sat down again and sipped her wine as George looked at the paper.

The army number he knew well; he had seen it before on several documents. Beneath it in block letters had been written: "SCHIRMER 6."

George considered it carefully for a moment or two, then nodded. He had not mentioned the name Schirmer to the Captain. Trickery was quite out of the question. The evidence was conclusive. What had happened afterwards to the body of Sergeant Schirmer might never be known, but there was no shadow of doubt that Madame Vassiotis and her mysterious acquaintance were telling what they knew of the truth.

He nodded and, picking up his glass of wine, raised it politely to the woman before he drank.

"Thank her for me, please, Miss Kolin," he said as he put the glass down, "and tell her that I am well satisfied."

He got out a fifty-dollar bill and put it on the table as he stood up.

He saw an expression of hastily concealed amazement flicker across the fat woman's face. Then she rose to her feet bowing and smiling. She was clearly delighted. If her dignity had permitted it she would have picked up the bill to have a closer look. She pressed them to have more wine.

When, eventually, they were able to bow themselves out of the shop, George turned to Miss Kolin. "You'd better tell her not to mention that fifty dollars to Monsieur Kliris," he said; "I shan't mention it to the Captain. With any luck she may get paid twice."

Miss Kolin was on her sixth after-dinner brandy, and her eyes were glazing rapidly. She was sitting very straight in her chair. At any moment now she would decide that it was time for her to go to bed. The captain had long since departed. He had had the air of a man of whose good nature unfair advantage had been taken. However, he had not refused the hundred dollars George had offered him. Presumably he was now celebrating the occasion with his mistress. For George, there was nothing more to be done in Florina.

"We'll leave tomorrow morning, Miss Kolin," he said. "Train to Salonika. Plane to Athens. Plane to Paris. All right?"

"You have definitely decided?"

"Can you think of one reason for going on with the thing?"

"I never had any doubt that the man was dead."

"No, that's right, you didn't. Going to bed now?"

"I think so, yes. Good night, Mr. Carey."

"Good night, Miss Kolin."

Watching her meticulous progress to the door of the café, George wondered gloomily if she kept her rigid self-control until she got into bed or whether, in the privacy of her room, she allowed herself to pass out.

He finished his own drink slowly. He felt depressed and wished to account for the fact. According to the lights of the ambitious young corporation lawyer who, only a few weeks back, had been pleased to watch his name being painted on an office door in Philadelphia, he should have been delighted by the turn of events. He had been given an irksome and unrewarding task and had performed it quickly and efficiently. He could now return with confidence to more serious and useful business. Everything was fine. And yet he was deriving no pleasure from the fact. It was absurd. Could it be that, in his heart, he had hoped, ludicrously, to find the Schneider Johnson claimant and take him back in triumph to that juvenile dotard, Mr. Sistrom? Could it be that what was now troubling him was merely an idiotic feeling of anticlimax? That must be it, of course. For a moment or two he almost succeeded in convincing himself that he had discovered the reason for his state of mind. Then the even less palatable truth of the matter dawned on him. He had been enjoying himself.

Yes, there it was. The talented, ambitious, pretentious Mr. Carey, with his smug, smiling family, his Brooks Brothers suits, and his Princeton and Harvard degrees, *liked* playing detectives, *liked* looking for non-existent German soldiers, *liked* having dealings with dreary people like Frau Gresser, disagreeable people like Colonel Chrysantos, and undesirables like Phengaros. And why? For the value of such experiences in a corporation law practice? Because he loved his fellow men and was curious about them? Rubbish. More likely that the elaborate defences of his youth, the pompous fantasies of big office chairs and panelled boardrooms, of hidden wealth and power behind the scenes, were beginning to crumble, and that the pimply adolescent was belatedly emerging into the light. Was it not possible that, in finding out something about a dead man, he had at last begun to find out something about himself?

He sighed, paid the bar bill, got his key, and went up to his room.

It was in the front of the hotel on the second floor, and at night the light streaming down from unshuttered windows across the street was almost strong enough to read by.

When he opened the door, therefore, he did not immediately look for the light switch. The first thing he saw as he took the key out of the lock was his briefcase lying open on the bed, with its contents scattered about the covers.

He started forward quickly. He had taken about two steps when the door slammed behind him. He swung around.

A man was standing just beside the door. He was in the shadow, but the pistol in his hand was clearly visible in the light from across the street. It moved forward as the man spoke.

He spoke very softly, but, even for George's scattered senses, the strong Cockney accent in the voice was unmistakable.

"All right, chum," it said. "Gently does it. No, don't move. Just put your hands behind your head, keep absolutely quiet, and hope you won't get hurt. Got it?"

9

GEORGE'S EXPERIENCE of extreme danger had been gained in the cockpits of heavy bombers and in circumstances for which he had been carefully prepared by long periods of training. Of dangers such as those which lurk behind doors in Macedonian hotels, dangers unrelated to the wearing of a uniform and the organized prosecution of a war, he had had no experience, and neither Princeton nor Harvard Law School had done anything to prepare him for one.

As, therefore, he raised his hands obediently and put them behind his head, he was suddenly aware of an overwhelming, unreasoning, and quite impracticable desire to run away somewhere and hide. He struggled against it for a moment; then the man spoke again and the desire went as suddenly as it had arrived. The blood began to pound unpleasantly in his head.

"That's right, chum," the voice was saying soothingly. "Now just go over to the window there and pull the shutters to. Then we'll have a little light on the scene. Slowly does it. Yes, you'll have to use your hands, but watch what you do with them or we'll have an accident. Don't try calling out or anything, either. All nice and quiet. That's the ticket."

George pulled the shutters to, and at the same moment the light in the room went on. He turned.

The man who stood by the light switch, watching him, was in his middle thirties, short and thickset, with dark, thinning hair. His suit was obviously a local product. Just as obviously he was not. The rawboned, snub-nosed face and the sly, insolent eyes originated,

126

as did the Cockney accent, from somewhere within the Greater London area.

"That's better, eh?" the visitor said. "Now we can see what's what without the neighbours across the street getting nosy."

"What the hell's the idea of all this?" said George. "And who the hell are you?"

"Easy, chum." The visitor grinned. "No names, no pack drill. You can call me Arthur if you like. It's not my name, but it'll do. Lots of people call me Arthur. You're Mr. Carey, aren't you?"

"You should know." George looked at the papers strewn over the bed.

"Ah, yes. Sorry about that, Mr. Carey. I meant to clear it up before you came back. But I didn't have time for more than a glance. I haven't taken anything, naturally."

"Naturally. I don't leave money in hotel rooms."

"Oh, what a *wicked* thing to say!" said the visitor skittishly. "Tongue like a whiplash, haven't we?"

"Well, if you're not here for money, what are you here for?"

"A bit of a chat, Mr. Carey. That's all."

"Do you usually come calling with a gun?"

The visitor looked pained. "Look, chum, how was I to know you'd be reasonable—finding a stranger in your room? Supposing you'd start yelling blue murder and throwing the furniture about. I had to take precautions."

"You could have asked for me downstairs."

The visitor grinned slyly. "Could I? Ah, but maybe you don't know much about these parts, Mr. Carey. All right"—his tone suddenly became businesslike—"I'll tell you what I'll do with you. You promise not to start calling up the management or getting Charlie with me, and I'll put the gun away. O.K.?"

"All right. But I'd still like to know what you're doing here."

"I told you. I want a little private chat. That's all."

"What about?"

"I'll tell you." Arthur put his gun away inside his

jacket and produced a packet of Greek cigarettes. He offered them to George. "Smoke, Mr. Carey?"

George produced a packet of his own. "No, thanks. I'll stick to these."

"Chesterfields, eh? Long time no see. Mind if I try one?"

"Help yourself."

"Thanks." He fussed about the business of giving George a light like an over-anxious host. Then he lit his own cigarette and drew on it appreciatively. "Nice tobacco," he said. "Very nice."

George sat down on the edge of the bed. "Look," he said impatiently, "what exactly is this all about? You break into my room, go through my business papers, threaten me with a gun, and then say you only want a private chat. All right, so we're chatting. Now what?"

"Mind if I sit down, Mr. Carey?"

"Do anything you like, but for Pete's sake come to the point."

"All right, all right, give us a chance." Arthur sat down gingerly on a cane-backed chair. "It's a private sort of a matter, Mr. Carey," he said. "Confidential, if you know what I mean."

"I know what you mean."

"I wouldn't like it to go any further," he persisted maddeningly.

"I've got that."

"Well now"—he cleared his throat—"I have been given to understand by certain parties," he said carefully, "that you, Mr. Carey, have been making certain inquires of a confidential nature in the town."

"Yes."

"This afternoon you had a certain conversation with a certain woman who shall be nameless."

"Madame Vassiotis, you mean?"

"That's right."

"Then why say she shall be nameless?"

"No names, no pack drill."

"Oh, all right. Get on."

"She gave you certain information."

"What about it?"

128

"Easy does it, Mr. Carey. Your inquiries were *re* a certain German N.C.O. named Schirmer. Correct?"

"Correct."

"Do you mind telling me why you are making the said inquiries, Mr. Carey?"

"If you were to tell me first just why you wanted to know, I might tell you."

Arthur digested this reply for a moment or two in silence.

"And, just to make matters simple, Arthur," George added, "I'll tell you that, although I'm a lawyer, I'm quite capable of understanding ordinary English. So what about letting your hair down and coming to the point?"

Mr. Arthur's low forehead creased with the effort of thinking. "You see, it's confidential, that's the trouble, Mr. Carey," he said unhappily.

"So you explained. But if it's so confidential that you can't talk about it, you'd better go home and let me get some sleep, hadn't you?"

"Now, don't talk like that, Mr. Carey. I'm doing my best. Look! If you were to tell me what you want to know about this chap for, I could tell certain persons who might be able to help you."

"What persons?"

"Persons with information to give."

"You mean information to *sell*, don't you?"

"I said *give*."

George examined his guest thoughtfully. "You're British, aren't you, Arthur?" he said after a moment. "Or is that confidential?"

Arthur grinned. "Want to hear me speak Greek? I speak it like a native."

"All right, then. You're a citizen of the world, then, eh?"

"Goldsmith!" said Arthur unexpectedly.

"Pardon?"

"Oliver Goldsmith," repeated Arthur; "he wrote a book called *The Citizen of the World*. We had it at school. Lot of crap about a Chinaman who comes to London and sees the sights."

129

"What part of London do you come from, Arthur?"

Arthur wagged a finger coyly. "Ah, naughty, naughty! That would be telling!"

"Afraid I'll check up on the British War Office lists of troops reported missing in Greece and find out which ones came from where you came from?"

"What do *you* think, chum?"

George smiled. "O.K., Arthur. Here it is. This man Schirmer I've been inquiring about was entitled to some money left by a distant relative of his in America. He was reported missing. I came here really to get information of his death, but I'd also like to know if he ever had any children. That's all. I found out today that he's dead."

"From old Ma Vassiotis?"

"That's right. And now I'm on my way home."

"I get it." Arthur was thinking hard now. "Much money, is there?" he said at last.

"Just enough to make it worth my while coming here."

"And that little bit of homework you've got with you?"

"Miss Kolin, you mean? She's an interpreter."

"I get you." Arthur came to a decision. "Supposing —just supposing, mind—that there was a bit more information you could find out about this German. Would it be worth your while to stay another couple of days?"

"That would depend on the information."

"Well, supposing he'd had a wife and kids. They'd be in line for the cash, wouldn't they?"

"*Did* he have a wife and kids?"

"I'm not saying he did and I'm not saying he didn't. But just supposing—"

"If there was clear, legal proof of that to be had, I'd certainly stay. But I'm not staying just in order to listen to a lot of unconfirmed hearsay, and I'm not paying out another cent to anyone."

"Nobody's asked you to, have they?"

"Not so far."

"Nasty suspicious nature you got, eh?"

"Yes."

Arthur nodded gloomily. "Can't blame you. Tricky lot of sods in this part of the world. Look, if I give you my sacred word of honour that it'll be worth your while to stay a couple of days, will you do it?"

"You're asking rather a lot aren't you?"

"Listen, chum. *You're* the one that's going to get a favour done. Not me!"

"That's what you say."

"Well, I can't do more. Here's the proposition. Take it or leave it. If you want the information my friends have got, stay here and do what I tell you."

"And what might that be?"

"Well, first of all, you don't say one word to that little bastard of a Captain you were chin-wagging with last night. O.K.?"

"Go on."

"All you do is go to that big café with the yellow blinds next door to the Acropolis Hotel between four and five tomorrow afternoon. Just sit there and have a cup of coffee. That's all. If you get no message from me while you're there, it's all off. If you do get a message, it'll be an appointment. Just say nothing and keep it."

"What about the interpreter?"

"If she keeps her mouth shut she can come too."

"Where would the appointment be?"

"You'd be taken to it by car."

"I see. Just one question. I'm not exactly timid, but I would like to know a bit more about these friends of yours before I do anything about meeting them. Would they be ELAS people, for instance?"

Arthur grinned. "Ask no qeustions and you'll be told no lies. You don't have to come if you don't want to."

"Maybe not. But I'm not half-witted. You say these friends of yours don't want money for their information. O.K., what do they want? For that matter, what do you want?"

"Sweet Fanny Adams," said Arthur cheerfully.

"Let's quit kidding."

"All right. Maybe they want to see justice done."

"Justice?"

131

"Yes. Ever heard of it?"

"Sure. I've heard of kidnapping too."

"Oh, blimey!" Arthur laughed. "Look, if you're as nervous as that, chum, forget it." He stood up. "I'll have to be getting along now. If you want to come, be at the café tomorrow like I said. Otherwise—" He shrugged.

"O.K. I'll think about it."

"Yes, you do that. Sorry to mess up all your papers like that, but I expect you'd sooner tidy them up yourself, really. Bye-bye for now."

"Good-bye," said George.

Almost before the word was out of his mouth, Arthur was out of the room and shutting the door noiselessly behind him.

It was not his uncertainty about bedbugs that kept George from sleeping soundly that night.

The café with the yellow blinds was in an exposed position on a busy corner, and everyone sitting in it could be clearly seen from anywhere in the main square. It was, George thought, the very last place he would have associated with the transaction of clandestine business. But then, he was not a practiced conspirator. The café's air of having nothing to conceal was probably its greatest asset. In Arthur's world, no doubt, such matters were elaborately calculated.

Miss Kolin had listened blandly to George's account of his interview with Arthur and accepted without comment his decision to postpone their departure. When, however, he had gone on to say that, in view of the possible risks involved, he would leave her to decide for herself whether she would accompany him or not, she had been quite obviously amused.

"Risks, Mr. Carey? But what sort of risks?"

"How should I know?" George was irritated. "The point is that this isn't exactly the most law-abiding part of the world and this guy Arthur's way of introducing himself for a cozy chat wasn't exactly according to Emily Post, was it?"

She had shrugged. "It served its purpose."

132

"What do you mean?"

"Frankly, Mr. Carey, I think that it was a mistake to give the Vassiotis woman so much money."

"From my point of view, she'd earned it."

"Your point of view, Mr. Carey, is that of an American lawyer. The point of view of the Vassiotis and her friends are different."

"I see. You think that this Arthur proposition is just another shakedown then?"

"I do. You gave that Captain a hundred dollars and the Vassiotis fifty. Now Mr. Arthur and his friends would like some dollars, too."

"He emphasized that there was no question of money involved. I told you."

"You believed him?"

"All right, then, I'm the prize sucker. But, for some reason, I did believe him. For some reason, equally idiotic no doubt, I still do."

She had shrugged again. "Then you are right to keep the appointment. It will be interesting to see what happens."

That had been over breakfast. By lunch-time his confidence in his first estimate of Arthur's intentions had completely evaporated. Sitting in the café with the yellow blinds, glumly sipping coffee, he had only one consoling thought in his head: no matter what happened, no matter what they did, neither Arthur nor any of Arthur's friends was going to get one red cent for his trouble.

It was after five o'clock now. The café was three parts empty. Nobody who looked as if he might conceivably have a message to deliver had been near them.

George finished his coffee. "All right, Miss Kolin," he said, "let's pay and go."

She signalled to the waiter. When his change came, George noticed a fold of grey paper underneath it. He put it in his pocket with the change. When they had left the café, he took out the paper and unfolded it.

The message was written in a careful schoolboy hand and in pencil:

A car with the registration number 19907 will be waiting for you outside the Cinema at 20.00 hrs. [it said]. *If anyone wants to know where you are going you are going for a drive to get some air. The driver is O.K. Ask no questions. Do what he tells you. Wear comfortable shoes. Arthur.*

The car was an old open Renault that George remembered having seen once before in the town. On that occasion it had been piled high with furniture. Now it was empty, and the driver stood beside it, cap in hand, gravely holding open the door for them. He was a fierce, sinewy old man with a long white moustache and skin like leather. He wore a patched shirt and a pair of old striped trousers belted in at the waist with lighting flex. The back of the car showed signs of having recently carried vegetables as well as furniture. The old man scooped up a handful of decaying stalks and threw them in the road before getting into his seat and driving off.

Soon they had left the town and were on a road with a signpost pointing to Vevi, a station on the railroad east of Florina.

It was getting dark now and the old man turned on a single headlight. He drove to save gasoline, coasting down the hills with the ignition switched off, and starting up again only just before the car rolled to a standstill. The battery was down, and when the motor was not running, the headlight dimmed until it was useless. With the disappearance of the last of the daylight, every descent became a hair-raising plunge into blackness. Fortunately, they met no other traffic, but after one particularly sickening moment George protested.

"Miss Kolin, tell him to go slower down the hills or keep the motor running for the light. He'll kill us if he's not careful."

The driver turned right round in his seat to reply.

"He says the moon will be up presently."

"Tell him to look where he's going, for God's sake!"

"He says that there is no danger. He knows the road well."

"All right, all right. Don't say any more. Let him keep his eyes on the road."

They had been driving for nearly an hour, and the promised moon had begun to rise, when the road joined another coming from the north. Ten minutes later they turned to the left and began a long, steady climb through the hills. They passed one or two isolated stone barns, then the road began to get steadily worse. Soon the car was bouncing and sliding along over a surface littered with loose stones and rocks. After a mile or two of this, the car suddenly slowed down, lurched across the road to avoid an axle-deep pot-hole, and stopped dead.

The lurch and the sudden stop flung George against Miss Kolin. For a moment he thought that the car had broken down; then, as they disentangled themselves, he saw that the driver was standing there with the door open, motioning them to get out.

"What's the idea?" George demanded.

The old man said something.

"He says that this is where we get out," reported Miss Kolin.

George looked round. The road was a narrow ledge of track running across a bleak hillside of thorn scrub. In the bright moonlight it looked entirely desolate. From the scrub there came a steady chorus of cicadas.

"Tell him we're staying right here until he takes us where we're supposed to go."

There was a torrent of speech when this was translated.

"He says that this is as far as he can take us. This is the end of the road. We must get out and walk on. Someone will meet us on the road beyond. He must wait here. Those are his orders."

"I thought he said it was the end of the road."

"If we will come with him he will show us that he speaks the truth."

"Wouldn't you prefer to wait here, Miss Kolin?"

"Thank you, no."

They got out and began to walk on.

For about twenty yards the old man walked ahead of them, explaining something and making large dramatic gestures; then he stopped and pointed.

They had indeed come to the end of the road; or, at least, to the end of that stretch of it. At some time a big stone culvert had carried a mountain stream beneath the roadbed. Now the remains of it lay in a deep boulder-strewn gully that the stream had cut for itself in the hillside.

"He says that it was blown up by the Germans and that the winter rains have made it bigger every year."

"Are we supposed to cross it?"

"Yes. The road continues on the other side and there we will be met. He will stay by the car."

"How far on the other side will we be met?"

"He does not know."

"That advice about comfortable shoes should have warned me. Well, I suppose that now we're here we may as well go through with it."

"As you wish."

The bed of the stream was dry and they were able to pick their way over the stones and between the boulders without much trouble. Clambering up on the far side, however, was less easy, as the gully was deeper there. The night was warm and George's shirt was clinging stickily to his body by the time he had helped Miss Kolin up to the road.

They stood for a moment getting their breath and looking back. The old man waved and went back to his car.

"How long do you think it would take us to walk back to Florina from here, Miss Kolin?" George asked.

"I think he will wait. He has not been paid yet."

"*I* didn't hire him."

"He will expect you to pay all the same."

"We'll see about that. We'd better do what he says, anyway."

They began to walk.

Except for the chirruping of the cicadas and the grating of their own footsteps, there was no sound on the road. Once they heard the faint tinkle of a distant sheep bell, but that was all. They had been walking steadily and in silence for some minutes when Miss Kolin spoke quietly.

"There is someone on the road ahead."

"Where? I can't see anyone."

"By those bushes we are coming to. He moved out of the shadow for a moment and I saw the moonlight on his face."

George felt his calves tightening as they walked on. He kept his eyes fixed on the bushes. Then he saw a movement in the shadows and a man stepped out into the road.

It was Arthur; but a rather different Arthur from the one George had talked to in the hotel. He wore breeches, a bush-shirt open at the neck, and a peaked cap. The thin pointed shoes had been replaced by heavy ankle boots. There was a pistol holster on the broad leather belt round his waist.

"Evening, chum," he said as they came up to him.

"Hullo," said George. "Miss Kolin, this is Arthur."

"Pleased to meet you, miss." The tone was humbly respectful, but George could see the shrewd, insolent eyes summing her up.

Miss Kolin nodded. "Good evening." Her hostility was clearly audible.

Arthur pursed his lips at the sound. "No trouble getting here, I hope, Mr. Carey?" he asked anxiously. He was suddenly like a week-end host apologizing for the inadequacies of the local train service.

"None to speak of. Will that old man wait for us?"

"Oh, you don't want to worry about him. Shall we go?"

"Sure. Where to?"

"It's not far. I've got transport. Just up the road here."

He led the way. They followed in silence. About a quarter of a mile further on, the road ended again. This time the obstruction was due to a landslide from the hill above, which had obliterated a section of about fifty yards. However, a narrow track had been beaten out over the debris, and they stumbled along this

137

cautiously until the road reappeared. That is, George and Miss Kolin stumbled; Arthur went forward as sure-footedly as if he were on a city street. He was waiting for them when they got back to the road.

"Only a little way now," he said.

They walked on for another quarter of a mile. There were tamarisks growing out of the hillside here, and the moonlight cast their distorted shadows across the road. Then the shadows became solid and Arthur slowed down. Parked on a section of road which was wide enough for a vehicle to turn was a small covered truck.

"Here we are, chums. You hop in the back."

He shone a flashlight below the tailboard as he spoke. "You first, miss. Now careful. We don't want to spoil the nylons, do we? See that stirrup there? Well, just put your foot——"

He broke off as Miss Kolin climbed easily into the back of the truck. "I have been in a British army truck before," she said coldly.

"*Have* you now, miss? Well, well! That's nice, isn't it? By the way," he went on as George followed her, "I'm going to have to do the canvas up. It'll be a bit warmish, I'm afraid, but we haven't got far to go."

George groaned. "Do you have to?"

"Afraid so, chum. My pals are a bit touchy about people knowing where they are. You know——security."

"This had better be worth while. All right. Let's get on."

George and Miss Kolin sat on two box-shaped fixtures in the body of the truck, while their escort lashed down the canvas flaps. When he had finished, they heard him get into the driver's seat and start up. The truck lurched off over the stones.

Arthur was a forceful driver and the truck bucked and swayed about fantastically. Inside, it was impossible to remain seated and they stood crouched under the canvas top, clinging to the metal supports. The air inside, which was soon mixed with exhaust fumes, became almost unbreathable. George was dimly aware of the truck turning several hairpin bends and he knew

138

they were climbing steeply, but he quickly lost all sense of direction. After ten minutes or more of excruciating discomfort, he was beginning to think that he would have to shout to Arthur to pull up, when, after yet another turn, the truck ran on to a comparatively smooth surface and stopped. A moment later the rear canvas was unlashed, moonlight and air streamed in, and Arthur's face appeared at the tailboard.

He grinned. "Bit bumpy, was it?"

"Yes."

They climbed out stiffly and found themselves standing on what had once been the flagged courtyard of a small house. All that remained of the house itself was a ruined wall and a pile of debris.

"ELAS boys did that," Arthur explained; "the other lot were using it as a stronghold. We go this way."

The ruined house was on the summit of a pine-clad hill. They followed Arthur along a track which led from the house down through the trees.

They walked silently over pine needles for about fifty yards, then Arthur halted.

"Wait a tick," he said.

They waited while he went on ahead. It was very dark under the trees and there was a strong smell of pine resin. After the atmosphere in the truck, the soft, cool air was delicious. A faint murmur of voices came from the darkness ahead.

"Did you hear that, Miss Kolin?"

"Yes. They were speaking Greek, but I could not distinguish the words. It sounded like a sentry challenging and receiving a reply."

"What do you make of all this?"

"I think we should have left word with someone where we were going."

"We didn't know where we were going, but I did what I could. If we're not back by the time the *femme de chambre* cleans my room in the morning, she'll find a letter addressed to the manager of my bureau. In it there's the number of that old man's car and a note of explanation for the Captain."

"That was wise, Mr. Carey. I have noticed something—" She broke off. "He's coming back."

Her hearing was very acute. Several seconds went by before George was able to hear the soft rustle of approaching footsteps.

Arthur appeared out of the darkness. "O.K., chums," he said. "Here we go. We'll have a bit of light on the scene in half a tick."

They followed him down the path. It was getting less steep now. Then, as it levelled off, Arthur switched on a flashlight and George saw the sentry leaning against a tree with his rifle under his arm. He was a thin, middle-aged man in khaki drill trousers and a ragged singlet. He watched them intently as they went by.

They were clear of the pine trees now and there was a house in front of them.

"Used to be a village down the hill there," said Arthur. "Wiped out by some of the boys. All flat except our place, and we had to patch that up a good bit. Left to rot, it was. Belonged to some poor bastard of a deviationist who got his throat cut." He had become the week-end host again, proud and fond of his house and wanting his guests to share his enthusiasm.

It was a two-story building with stuccoed walls and broad overhanging eaves. The shutters over the windows were all closed."

There was another sentry by the door. Arthur said something to him and the man shone a light on their faces before nodding to Arthur and motioning them on. Arthur opened the door and they followed him into the house.

There was a long narrow hall with a staircase and several doorways. An oil lamp hung from a hook by the front door. There was no plaster on the ceiling and very little left on the walls. It looked like what it was, a house which had been gutted by bomb blast or shellfire and temporarily repaired.

"Here we are," said Arthur: "H.Q. mess and anteroom."

He had opened the door of what appeared to be a dining-room. There was a bare trestle table with

140

benches on either side. On the table there were bottles, glasses, a pile of knives and forks, and another oil lamp. In a corner of the room, on the floor, there were empty bottles.

"Nobody at home," said Arthur. "I dare say you could do with a snifter, eh? Help yourselves. The you-know-what is just across the hall on the right if anybody's interested. I'll be back in a jiffy."

George looked at the bottles. There was Greek wine and plum brandy. He looked at Miss Kolin.

"Drink, Miss Kolin?"

"Yes, please."

He poured out two brandies. She picked hers up, drank it down at a gulp, and held the glass out to be filled again. He filled it.

"Pretty strong stuff this, isn't it?" he said tentatively.

"I hope so."

"Well, I didn't expect to be taken to a place like a military headquarters. What do you think it is?"

"I have an idea." She lit a cigarette. "You remember four days ago in Salonika there was a bank robbery?"

"I remember something about it. Why?"

"Next day, in the train to Florina, I read the newspaper reports of it. It gave an exact description of the truck that was used."

"What about it?"

"We came here in that truck tonight."

"What? You're kidding."

"No." She drank some more brandy.

"You're mistaken then. After all, there must be dozens, hundreds maybe, of these British army trucks still about in Greece."

"Not with slots for false number-plates."

"What do you mean?"

"I noticed the slots when he was shining the flashlight for me to get in. The false plates were on the floor in the back of the truck. When we stopped, I put them where the moonlight would shine as we got out. The part of the number I could see was the same as the one in the newspaper report."

"Are you absolutely sure?"

141

"I do not like it any more than you, Mr. Carey."

But George was remembering something that Colonel Chrysantos has said: *"They are clever and dangerous and the police do not catch them."*

"If they get half a suspicion we know anything—" he began.

"Yes. It could be most disagreeable." She raised her glass to drink again and then stopped.

There was the sound of footsteps coming down the stairs.

George drank his brandy down quickly and got out a cigarette. The learned judge, whose secretary he had been, had once said that it was impossible to practise law for very many years without learning that no case, however matter-of-fact it might seem, could be considered entirely proof against the regrettable tendency of reality to assume the shape and proportions of melodrama. At the time, George had smiled politely and wondered if he would be given to making such half-baked generalizations when *he* became a judge. Now he remembered.

The door opened.

The man who came into the room was fair and deep-chested, with heavy shoulders and big hands. He might have been any age between thirty and forty. The face was strong, with muscular cheeks, a determined mouth, and cool, watchful eyes. He held himself very erect and the bushshirt he wore stretched tightly across his chest. With the revolver belt at his waist he looked almost as if he were in uniform.

He glanced swiftly from George to Miss Kolin as Arthur, who had followed him in, shut the door and bustled forward.

"Sorry to keep you waiting," Arthur said. "Mr. Carey, this is my chief. He speaks a bit of English— I taught him—but go easy on the long words. He knows who you are."

The newcomer clicked his heels and gave the slightest of bows.

"Schirmer," he said curtly, "Franz Schirmer. I think you wish to speak with me."

142

10

THE GERMAN forces which withdrew from Greece in October 1944 were very different in both numbers and quality from the field army which had invaded the country just over three years earlier. If the Twelfth Army of General von List, with its crack panzer divisions and its record of success in the Polish campaign, had epitomized the irresistible strength of the *Wehrmacht,* the occupation forces, setting out to make their way home while there was still a road home left open to them, epitomized no less strikingly the *Wehrmacht*'s ultimate exhaustion. The earlier practice of resting troops from the fighting fronts by giving them tours of occupation duty had long been abandoned as a luxury. The Lines of Communication Division which garrisoned the Salonika area in 1944 was, for the most part, made up of men who, for one reason or another, were considered unfit for combatant duty: debilitated survivors from the Russian front, the older men, the weaklings, and those who, because of either wounds or sickness, were of low medical categories.

For Sergeant Schirmer, the war had ended on that day in Italy when he had obeyed the order of an inexperienced officer to make a parachute jump over a wood. The comradeship of fighting men in a *corps d'élite* has meant a great deal to a great many men. To Sergeant Schirmer it had given something that his upbringing had always denied him—his belief in himself as a man. The months in the hospital which had followed the accident, the court of inquiry, the rehabilitation center, the medical examinations, and the posting to Greece had been a bitter epilogue to the only period of his life in which he felt he had known happiness. Many times he had wished that the tree branch which had merely broken his hip had pierced his breast and killed him.

If the Ninety-fourth Garrison Regiment at Salonika had been the kind of unit in which a soldier like Sergeant Schirmer could have come to take even a grudging pride, many things no doubt would have been very different. But it was not a unit in which any self-respecting man could have taken pride. The officers (with a few exceptions such as Lieutenant Leubner) were the army's unemployables, the kind of officers whom unit commanders hasten to get rid of when they have the chance and who spend most of their service lives held on depot establishments awaiting postings. The N.C.O.'s (again with a few exceptions) were incompetent and corrupt. The rank and file were a disgruntled and decrepit assembly of old soldiers, chronic invalids, dullards, and petty delinquents. Almost the first order which the Sergeant had received from an officer on joining had been an order to remove his paratrooper's badge. That had been his introduction to the regiment, and as time went by, he had learned to fortify and console himself with his contempt for it.

The German withdrawal from Thrace was an ignominious affair. The depot soldiers responsible for the staff work had had little experience of moving troops in the field and still less of supplying them while they were on the move. Units like the Ninety-fourth Garrison Regiment, and there was more than one, could do little to make good the deficiencies. The knowledge that British raiding forces were advancing rapidly from the south in order to harass the retreat, and that *andarte* bands were already hovering aggressively on the flanks, may have lent urgency to the withdrawal, but, in doing so, it had also added to the confusion. It was traffic congestion rather than any brilliant planning by Phengaros that led to the ambushing of Sergeant Schirmer's convoy.

He was one of the last of his regiment to leave the Salonika area. Contempt for his regiment he might have, but that did not prevent his doing his utmost to see that the fraction of it that he controlled carried out its orders properly. As headquarters weapons-instructor, he had no platoon responsibilities and came under the command of an engineer officer in charge of a special rear-guard party. This officer was Lieutenant Leubner, and he had been detailed to carry out a series of important demolitions in the wake of the retreat.

The Sergeant liked Lieutenant Leubner, who had lost a hand in Italy; he felt that the Lieutenant understood him. Between them they organized the party in two detachments, and the Sergeant was given command of one of them.

He drove his men and himself unmercifully and succeeded in completing his part of the work in accordance with the timetable issued with the movement order. During the night of the 23rd of October his detachment loaded the trucks they were to take with them and moved out of Salonika. They were exactly on schedule.

His orders were to go through Vodena, deal with the gasoline dump on the Apsalos road, and then rendezvous with Lieutenant Leubner at the bridge by Vodena. It had been anticipated that the laying of the demolition charges for the bridge would call for the united efforts of the two detachments if it were to be done to schedule. The time of the rendezvous had been fixed for dawn.

At first light that day Sergeant Schirmer was at Yiannitsa, only a little over halfway along the road to Vodena, and trying desperately to force a way for his detachment past a column of tank transporters. The transporters should have been fifty miles further on, but had themselves been held up by a column of horse-drawn wagons which had debouched from the Naoussa road twelve hours behind schedule. The Sergeant was two hours late when he passed through Vodena. Had he been on time, Phengaro's men would have missed him by an hour.

It had rained during the night, and with the rising sun the air became stiflingly humid; moreover, the Sergeant had had no sleep for thirty hours. Yet, as he sat beside the driver of the leading truck, he had little difficulty in staying awake. The machine-pistol lying across his knees reminded him of the need for vigilance, and the dull pain of his overworked hip prevented his settling into too comfortable a position. But his fatigue manifested itself in other ways. His eyes, scouring an area of hillside above the bend in the road towards which they were climbing, kept shifting focus suddenly, so that he had to shake his head before he could see properly; and his thoughts wandered with dreamlike inconsequence from the problems of the task in hand, and the possible plight of Lieutenant Leubner's detachment, to the attack on Eben-Emael, to a girl he had had in Hanover, and then, uneasily, to the moment in Salonika forty-eight hours earlier when Kyra had wept as he had said good-bye to her.

The weeping of women always made the Sergeant feel uneasy. It was not that he was sentimental where women were concerned; it was simply that the sound of weeping always seemed to presage his own misfortunes. There had been the time in Belgium, for instance, when that old woman had stood bleating because they had killed her cow. Two days after that he had been wounded. There had been the time in Crete when it had been necessary for discipline to put some of the married men up against a wall and shoot them. A month later, in Benghazi, he had gone down with dysentery. There had been the time in Italy when some of the lads had fooled about with a young girl. Two days before his jumping accident, *that* had been. He would never admit to such an unreasoning and childish superstition, of course; but if he ever married, it would be to some girl who would not weep even if he beat the living daylights out of her. Let her scream as much as she liked, let her try and kill him if she wanted to, and dared, but let there be no weeping. It meant bad luck.

It was the off-side front wheel of the truck that exploded the mine. The Sergeant felt the lift of it a split second before his head hit the canopy of the driver's cab.

Then, there was something wet on his face and a thin, high singing in his ears. He was lying face-downwards and everything was dark except for one winking disk of light. Something gave him a violent blow in the side, but he was too tired to cry out or even to feel pain. He could hear men's voices and knew that they were speaking Greek. Then the sounds of their voices faded and he began to fall through the air towards the trees below, defending himself against the cruel branches by locking his ankles tightly and pointing his toes, as he had been taught in the parachute jumping school. The trees engulfed him with a sigh that seemed to come from his own lips.

When he regained consciousness for the second time, there seemed to be nothing wet on his face, but something stretching the skin of it. The disk of light was still there, but it no longer winked. He became aware now of his arms stretched out above his head, as if he were going to dive into water. He could feel his heart beating, sending pain from all over his body into his head. His legs felt warm. He moved his fingers and they dug into grit and pebbles. Consciousness began to flood back. There was something the matter with his eyelids and he could not see properly, but he kept looking at the disk of light and moved his head slightly. Suddenly, he realized that the disk was a small white pebble lying in a patch of sunlight. Then he remembered that he was in Greece and had been in a truck that had been hit. With an effort, he rolled on to his side.

The force of the explosion had overturned the truck and smashed the floor of it to matchwood, but the main blast had missed the driver's cab. The Sergeant had been lying in an oil-drenched litter of empty gasoline cans and debris, with his face in the mess of blood which had poured from his head wound. The blood had congealed now on his cheeks and in his eyes. The wreckage of the truck hung over him, shading all but his legs from the sun. There was no sound except the chirping of cicadas and faint dripping noises from the truck.

He began to move his limbs. Though he knew that he had hurt his head, he did not as yet know the extent of his injuries. His great fear was that his hip

147

had broken again. For several long seconds all he could think of was the X-Ray picture the surgeon had shown him of the thick metal pin which had been inserted to strengthen the neck of the damaged bone. If that had been torn away, he was finished. He moved the leg carefully. The hip was very painful, but it had been painful before the mine had exploded. Fatigue always made it painful. He became bolder and, drawing the leg up under him, began to sit up. It was then that he noticed that all his equipment had gone. He remembered the Greek voices and the blow he had felt and began to realize what had happened.

His head was throbbing horribly, but the hip seemed to be all right. He dragged himself to his knees. A moment later he vomited. The effort exhausted him and he lay down again to rest. He knew that the head wound might be serious. It was not the amount of the bleeding that concerned him—he had seen plenty of scalp wounds and knew that they bleed profusely—but the possibility of there being internal bleeding from the concussion. However, he would know soon enough if there were, and there was, in any case, nothing he could do about it. His immediate task was to find out what had happened to the rest of the detachment and, if possible, take steps to deal with the situation. He made another effort to get to his feet and, after a bit, succeeded.

He looked about him. His watch had gone, but the position of the sun told him that less than an hour had elapsed since the crash. The wreckage of the truck lay across the road, completely blocking it. The body of the driver was nowhere to be seen. He moved out cautiously into the middle of the road and looked down the hill.

The second truck had stopped slewed across the road a hundred yards away. Three German soldiers lay in the road by it. Beyond he could just see the canopy of the driver's cab belonging to the third truck. He set off slowly down the hill, pausing every now and then to get his strength. The sun beat down and the flies buzzed round his head. It seemed an enormous distance to the second truck. He began to feel that he was going to vomit again, and lay down in the shade of a bush to recover. Then he went on.

The soldiers in the road were quite dead. One of them, who looked as if he had first been wounded by a grenade burst, had his throat cut. All the arms and equipment had been taken, but the contents of two haversacks were strewn on the ground. The truck had some bullet holes in it and was scarred by grenade bursts, but it seemed all right otherwise. For several wild moments he considered turning it round and driving back to Vodena, but the road was not wide enough to turn in and he knew that, even if it had been, he would not have had the strength to do the job.

He could see the third truck plainly now, and with it more dead men. One of them was hanging over the side of it, his arms dangling grotesquely. It seemed probable that the whole of his detachment had become casualties. In any case, there was little point in investigating further. Militarily speaking, it had certainly ceased to exist. It would be in order for him, then, to look to his own safety.

He leaned against the side of the truck to rest again and caught sight of his face in the driving mirror. The blood had congealed all over his hair as well as in his eyes and on his face; his whole head looked as inhuman as if it had been smashed to a pulp; it was easy to see why the *andartes* had taken him for dead.

His heart leaped suddenly with fear and sent a shaft of pain to the top of his head. The *andartes* had gone for the moment, but there was more than a possibility that they would return with drivers for the two serviceable trucks. It was even possible that they had left a sentry, and that, somewhere on the hillside above, the sights of a rifle were being steadied on him at that very moment. But at the same moment reason told him that there was very probably no sentry, and that, even if there were, the man had already had more than enough time to shoot if he had intended to do so.

Nevertheless, the place was dangerous. Whether the *andartes* returned or whether they did not, it would not be very long before the local inhabitants ventured on the scene. There were still plenty of pickings for them; the boots of the dead, the gasoline cans, the tires on the trucks, the tool kits. The *andartes* had taken scarcely anything. He would have to get away quickly.

For a moment or two he thought of trying to go ahead on foot in the hope of reaching the fuel dump, but he soon abandoned the idea. Even if he had had enough strength to walk that distance, the chance of his being able to do so in broad daylight unseen by the local inhabitants would be remote. In that area and at that time, a solitary German soldier, wounded and un-armed, would be lucky if he were not tortured before he was stoned to death by the women. The road back to Vodena would be even more dangerous. He must wait for darkness, therefore; and that might give him time to recover his strength too. His immediate course of action, then, was plain enough; he must find water, food, and a place to hide. Later on, if he were still alive, he would decide what to do next.

The water bottles had all been taken. He dragged an empty gasoline can out of the truck and began to drain the radiator into it. When it was half full he realized that he would not have the strength to carry more. There was still plenty left in the radiator, and it was not too hot to drink now. When he had slaked his thirst, he soaked his handkerchief in the water and sponged the blood from his face and eyes. His head he did not touch for fear of starting the bleeding again.

Next he looked for food. The *andartes* had taken the sack with the supplies in it, but he knew the ways of army truckdrivers, and went to the tool-box. There were two emergency rations there, some sticks of chocolate, and the driver's greatcoat. He put the rations and the chocolate in the greatcoat pocket and slung it over his shoulder. Then he picked up the can of water and limped back slowly up the road.

He had already decided on his hiding-place. He re-membered how innocent the hillside above had looked when he had been coming up the road in the truck, and how well it had concealed the attackers. It would conceal him in the same way. He left the road and started to climb.

It took him half an hour to climb a hundred yards. Once he lay for nearly ten minutes, too exhausted to move, before he could bring himself to crawl painfully on. The hillside was very steep and he had to drag the heavy water can behind him. Several times he thought of leaving it and returning later to pick it up, but some instinct warned him that water was more necessary to him now than food and that he could not risk losing it. He crawled on until at last he could go no farther and lay for a time retching helplessly, unable even to crawl out of the sun. Flies began to settle on his face without his being able to brush them away. After a while, tortured by the flies, he opened his eyes to see where he was.

There was a clump of thorn bushes a yard or so away, with a tamarisk growing among them. With a tremendous effort he dragged the can of water into the the shade of the tree and crawled in among the thorn bushes with the greatcoat. The last thing he saw was a column of dense black smoke rising from somewhere beyond the hill in the direction of the fuel dump. Then, realizing that one at least of his decisions had been made for him, he lay face-downwards on the coat and slept.

It was dark when he awoke. The pain in his head was agonizing, and although the night was warm, he was shivering violently. He crawled to the can of water and dragged it nearer to his bed. He knew now that he had a bout of malaria to add to his troubles and to reduce his resistance to a possible infection of the head wound. He might be going to die, but the knowledge did not trouble him. He would fight for life as long as he was able. If he were defeated, it would not matter. He had done the best he could.

He lay among the thorn bushes for nearly four days. For most of the time he was in a sort of half-waking dream state, dimly aware of the changes from darkness to light, but of little else that was outside him. At some moments, he would know with one bit of his mind that he was delirious and talking to people who were not there; at others, he would be lost in the recurrent nightmare of the fall through the trees, which never seemed to end twice in the same way.

On the third day, he awoke from a deep sleep to find that the pain in his head had lessened, that he could think clearly, and that he felt hungry. He ate part of one of the emergency rations and then inspected his water supply. The can was nearly empty, but there was enough to last for that day. For the first time since he had crawled up the hill, he got to his feet. He felt horribly weak, but he forced himself to walk out of his hiding-place and look down at the road.

The two serviceable trucks had disappeared and, to his astonishment, the damaged one had been set on fire and burned out. The charred wreckage of it looked like a black stain on the limestone grit of the road. He had neither seen nor heard anything of this bonfire.

He went back to his hiding-place and slept again. Once, during the night, he awoke to the sound of many planes flying overhead and knew that the final stage of the withdrawal had been reached. The *Luftwaffe* was evacuating the Yidha airfield. He lay awake for a time listening and feeling very much alone, but eventually he went back to sleep. The following morning he felt stronger and was able to go in search of water. He kept away from the road and, about half a mile down the hill, found a stream, in which he washed after replenishing his drinking-water supply.

He had crossed a terraced vineyard to get to the stream, and on his way back he almost ran into a man and a woman working there. However, he saw them just in time and, retracing his steps, made his way round the vineyard. In doing so, he came near the road and found the seven freshly dug graves, with a steel helmet and a cairn on each. There was a stake driven into the ground with a note fastened to it giving the number and names of those buried there and asking that the site should not be disturbed. It was signed by Lieutenant Leubner.

Sergeant Schirmer was strangely moved. It had not once occurred to him that the Lieutenant might find time to interest himself in the fate of the lost detachment. No doubt it had been he who had burned the damaged truck and removed the others. A good officer, the Lieutenant.

He looked at the note again. Seven dead. That meant that three, including the missing driver, had been made prisoner or escaped. The paper was already somewhat tattered and it had probably been there for over two days. It was bitter to know that friendly hands had been so near while he had lain hidden and oblivious among the thorn bushes. For the first time since the mine had exploded he was conscious of a feeling of despair.

He thrust it away angrily. What had he to despair of? His inability to rejoin the Ninety-fourth Garrison Regiment, fumbling its way back to the Fatherland with its tail between its legs? The lack of someone to ask for orders? How the instructors at the parachute training school would have laughed!

He looked down again at the graves. He had no cap or helmet and so could not salute. He drew himself up into the position of attention and clicked his heels respectfully. Then he picked up his water can and made his way back to the hillside and the thorn bushes.

After he had finished the remains of the first emergency ration, he lay down to think things out.

The expedition for water had tired him sufficiently for him to realize that he was still very weak. Another twenty-four hours must elapse before he was fit to move. The food he had left could probably be made to last that long. After that he must forage.

And then what?

The German forces had probably left Vodena two days or more ago. It was idle to suppose that he could catch up with them now. He would have hundreds of miles of difficult country to travel before he could do that. His only chance of getting through unseen would be to avoid the roads; yet if he did that, the long, hard marches would soon lame him. He could try the railroad, of course, but that was almost certainly in the

153

hands of the Greeks again by now. His despair returned, and this time it was not so easily dismissed. The plain fact was that there was nowhere he could reasonably go. He was completely cut off in hostile territory where capture or surrender meant death and the ways of escape were all closed. The only thing he could do, it seemed, was to go on living under the thorn bush like an animal, stealing what food he could from the fields. An escaped prisoner of war would be in a better position; at least he would have had time to prepare for the venture. He, Schirmer, was relatively helpless. He had no civilian clothes, no money, no papers, no food worth speaking of; moreover, he was still suffering from the after-effects of being blown up by a mine and an attack of malaria. He needed time to recover completely and time to plan. Above all, he needed someone to help him get identity papers. Clothes and money he might steal, but to steal papers printed in a language he could not read, and risk using them as his own, would be folly.

And then he thought of Kyra; Kyra, who had wept so bitterly when he had had to say good-bye to her, who had implored him, foolishly, to desert; the one friend he possessed in this hostile, treacherous land.

She had a small photographic processing business in Salonika. He had seen the bold AGFA advertisement sign outside her shop one day and gone in to see if he could buy some film for his camera. She had had no film to sell—it had been hard to come by at the time—but he had been attracted by her and had returned to the shop whenever he had had time off. There was little processing work to be had and to make more money she had set up a small curtained "studio" for the taking of identity-card and passport photographs. When a local military identity card had been issued to the occupation forces, he had been able to suggest to the officer responsible for the issue in his own unit, that she should be commissioned to do all the photographic work. He had also brought her army food. She lived with her brother in two rooms over the shop. However, the brother was a night duty clerk in a hotel which

had been commandeered by the occupation headquarters, and was only at home in the daytime. Quite
soon the Sergeant had been able to apply for a sleeping-
out pass. Kyra was a full-blooded young woman with
simple and readily fulfillable demands to make. The
Sergeant was both lusty and skillful. The relationship
had proved most satisfactory.

Now it could be made to serve another purpose.

Salonika was seventy-four kilometres away by road.
That meant that he would have to cover at least a
hundred kilometres in order to keep away from the
towns and villages. If he marched in daylight it would
probably take him about four days to get there. If he
played for safety and moved only at night, it would take
much longer. He must not work his hip too hard. He
must allow, too, for the time he would have to spend
getting food. The sooner he started, the better. His
spirits rose. The following night, having eaten the last
of the army rations and with only the chocolate in his
pocket for emergencies, he set off.

It took him eight days to reach his destination.
Travelling at night, without map and compass to guide
him, had proved too difficult. He had lost himself re-
peatedly. After the third night he had decided that he
must accept the greater risk and travel by day. He had
found it easier than he expected. Even in the plain,
there was plenty of cover to move in, and it had been
possible, except in the vicinity of Yiannitsa, to keep
fairly close to the road. Food was the greatest difficulty.
From an isolated farm he was able to steal some eggs,
and on another day he milked a straying goat; but
mostly he lived on the wild fruit he could pick. It was
not until the end of the seventh day that he decided
that the situation had become desperate enough for
him to eat his chocolate.

It was about ten o'clock in the morning when he
reached the outskirts of Salonika. He was near the
railroad and in an area that offered reasonable opportunities for concealment. He decided to stop there
and wait until nightfall before entering the city.

Now that his journey was nearly done, the thing

that most concerned him was his appearance. The wound on his scalp was healing well and would not excite much curiosity. He disliked the stubble of beard he had grown, but only because it was unsoldierly; he did not think that it would make him too conspicuous. The trouble was his uniform. It seemed to him that to walk through the streets of Salonika in a German uniform now would be to invite arrest or assassination. Something would have to be done.

He moved nearer to the railroad and began to reconnoitre along it. Eventually he came upon what he was looking for—a trackwalker's hut. It was padlocked, but there were some heavy iron rail-chairs on the ground near by and he used one to small the hasp through which the padlock was fastened.

He had hoped to find a pair of overalls or a workman's blouse of some sort in the hut, but there was no clothing there of any kind. There was, however, a workman's dinner wrapped in a sheet of newspaper; a piece of bread, some olives, and half a bottle of wine.

He took it back to his hiding-place and swallowed it greedily. The wine made him drowsy and he slept for a while afterwards. When he awoke, he felt much refreshed and began to reconsider the problem of his clothing.

He had on a grey cotton singlet under his tunic. If he discarded the tunic and belted his uniform trousers, the top part of him would look like a dock labourer. At night, when the colour and material of the trousers could not be seen clearly, the only things that would give him away would be his jackboots. He tried to conceal them by wearing the trousers over the boots instead of tucked inside them. The result was not altogether satisfactory, but he decided that it was sufficiently so. The risks he would have to run to steal clothing were probably greater than the risk of having his boots identified in the darkness. So far, good fortune had been with him. It would be foolish to try it too hard within sight of his objective.

By eight o'clock that night it was quite dark and he set off for the city.

He had a disagreeable surprise when he reached it. The quarters through which he had to pass were ablaze with lights. The citizens of Salonika were celebrating their liberation from the occupation forces and the arrival of the "Macedonian Group of Divisions" of ELAS.

It was a fantastic scene. Along the waterfront, long chains of screaming, singing people swayed and capered to music blaring from cafés and bars. The restaurants were jammed. Shrieking mobs danced on the chairs and tables. Everywhere there were groups of drunken *andartes,* many of them Bulgars, staggering about, shouting wildly, firing rifles into the air, and fetching women out of the brothels to dance with them in the streets. To the Sergeant, hurrying along discreetly in what shadows he could find, the city seemed like some vast orgiastic fairground.

Kyra's shop was in a narrow street near the Eski Juma. There were no bars or cafés in it and it was relatively quiet. The shopkeepers with shutters had taken the precaution of putting them up; others had nailed boards across their windows. Kyra's windows were protected in this way and the shop was in darkness; but there was a light in the window above it.

He was relieved at this. He had feared that she might be out taking part in the carnival in the streets, and that he would have to wait for her return. The fact that she was in also meant that she did not share in the popular rejoicing at the turn of events. That was all to the good.

He looked round carefully to see that his arrival had not been witnessed by anyone who might know him by sight; then, satisfied on this point, he rang the bell.

After a moment or two he heard her come down the stairs and cross the shop to the door. The boards prevented his seeing her. He heard her stop, but the door did not open.

"Who is it?" she said in Greek.

"Franz."

"God in heaven!"

"Let me in."

157

He heard her fumbling with the bolts and then the door opened. He stepped inside, shut the door quickly behind him, and took her in his arms. He could feel her trembling as he kissed her, and then she pressed away from him with a gasp of fear.

"What are you doing here?"

He told her what had happened to him and what he planned.

"But you cannot stay."

"I have to."

"No, you cannot."

"Why not, my beloved? There is no risk."

"I am already suspect because I have loved a German."

"What can they do?"

"I may be arrested."

"Absurd. If they arrested every woman in this place who has loved a German, they would need an army to guard them."

"It is different with me. The *andartes* have arrested Niki."

"What for?" Niki was her brother.

"He is accused of spying for the Germans and informing. When he has confessed and accused others, they will kill him."

"The swine! Nevertheless, I must stay, beloved."

"You must surrender. You would be a prisoner of war."

"Don't you believe it. They would cut my throat."

"No. There are many German soldiers here. Deserters. No harm comes to them if they say they are sympathizers."

"If they say they are Communists, you mean?"

"What does it matter?"

"You class me with these deserter swine?"

"Of course not, beloved. I wish only to save you."

"Good. First I need food. Then a bed. I will use Niki's room tonight. I am fit for nothing but sleep."

"But you cannot stay here, Franz. You cannot." She began to sob.

He gripped her arms. "No tears, my beloved, and

no arguments. You understand? I give the orders. When I have eaten and rested, then we can talk. Now, you can show me what there is to eat."

He had driven his fingers deep into her arm muscles, and when she stopped weeping he knew that he had frightened as well as hurt her. That was as it should be. There would be no more disobedience for the present.

They went up to the apartment. When she saw him in the light, she gave a cry of dismay, but he cut short her further lamentations impatiently.

"I am hungry," he said.

She put together a meal for him and watched him while he ate it. She was silent now and thoughtful, but he scarcely noticed her. He was planning. First he would sleep, and then he would see about getting a civilian suit. It was a pity that her brother Niki was so undersized; his clothes would be far too small. She would have to buy a second-hand suit somewhere. Then she could find out exactly what papers he would need in order to move about freely. There was the language difficulty, of course; but perhaps he could overcome that by pretending to be a Bulgar or an Albanian; there would be plenty of that sort of scum about now. After that, he would have to decide where to go. It would be an awkward problem. There were not many countries left in which a German soldier would be welcomed and assisted to repatriate himself. There was Spain, of course—he might get there by sea —or Turkey. . . .

But his head was drooping on his chest, and his eyes would no longer stay open. He roused himself sufficiently to go into the bedroom. At the bed he turned and looked back. Kyra was standing in the door watching him. She smiled reassuringly. He sank down on the bed and went to sleep.

It was still dark, and he could not have been asleep for much more than two hours, when he awoke in response to a violent shaking of his arm and a blow in the back.

He rolled over and opened his eyes.

Two men with pistols in their hands were standing

looking down at him. They wore the elementary kind of uniform which he had seen on the *andartes* rioting about in the streets a few hours earlier. Those, however, had all been very drunk; these were very sober and businesslike. They were lean, sour-looking young men with smart belts and brassards on their arms. He guessed that they were *andarte* officers. One of them spoke sharply in German.

"Get up."

He obeyed slowly, overcoming a longing for sleep more desperate than any sensation of fear. He hoped that they would kill him quickly so that he could rest.

"Your name?"

"Schirmer."

"Rank?"

"Sergeant. Who are you?"

"You'll find out. She says you were a paratrooper and an instructor. Is that correct?"

"Yes."

"Where did you win your Iron Cross?"

The Sergeant was sufficiently awake now to appreciate the necessity of lying. "In Belgium," he said.

"Do you want to live?"

"Who doesn't?"

"Fascists don't. They are death-lovers, so we kill them. True democrats want to live. They prove their desire by fighting with their class comrades against the Fascists and the capitalist-imperialist aggressors."

"Who are these aggressors?"

"Reactionaries and their Anglo-American bosses."

"I don't know anything about politics."

"Naturally. You have had no chance of learning about them. They are simple enough, however. Fascists die, true democrats live. You can, of course, choose freely which you are to be, but as time is short and there is much work to be done, you can have only twenty seconds to make up your mind. The usual time allowed is ten seconds, but you are an N.C.O., a skilled soldier, and a valuable instructor. Also you are not a deserter. You are entitled to think carefully before you accept the sacred responsibility which is offered to you."

"If I claim the rights of a prisoner of war?"

"You are no prisoner, Schirmer. You have not surrendered. You are still in the thick of the fight. At present you are an enemy of Greece, and"—the *andarte* raised his pistol—"we have much to avenge."

"And if I accept?"

"You will be given an early opportunity of demonstrating your political reliability, your loyalty, and your skill. The twenty seconds have long ago departed. What do you wish to say?"

The Sergeant shrugged. "I accept."

"Then salute," the *andarte* said sharply.

For an instant the Sergeant's right arm started to move, and in that instant he saw the *andarte*'s finger tighten on the trigger. He clenched the fist of his left hand and raised it above his head.

The *andarte* smiled thinly. "Very good. You may come with us in a moment." He went to the bedroom door and opened it. "But first there is another matter to attend to."

He beckoned Kyra into the room. She walked stiffly, her face a tear-stained mask of fear. She did not look at the Sergeant.

"This woman," the *andarte* said with a smile, "was good enough to inform us that you were here. Her brother was a Fascist-collaborationist spy. Her object in betraying you was to convince us that she has a true democratic spirit. What do you think about that, Comrade Schirmer?"

"I think she is a Fascist bitch," said the Sergeant shortly.

"Excellent. That was my own thought. You will learn fast."

The *andarte* glanced at his companion and nodded.

The companion's gun jerked up. Before Kyra could scream or the Sergeant could even think of protesting, three shots had crashed out. The shock waves brought down a small piece of plaster from the ceiling. The Sergeant felt it tap his shoulder as he saw the girl, her mouth still open, slammed against the wall by the force of the heavy bullets. Then she sank to the floor without a sound.

The *andarte* officers looked at her intently for a moment, then nodded again and walked out of the room.

The Sergeant followed. He knew that sometime when he was not so tired and confused he would feel horror at what had just happened. He had liked Kyra.

Sergeant Schirmer served in the Democratic Army of General Markos for just over four years.

After the December rebellion of '44 and the promotion of Markos to the command of the army, he had been sent to Albania. There, he had been an instructor in a training camp set up to discipline the guerrilla bands then being organized in larger formations, in preparation for the campaign of '46. It was in this camp that he met Arthur.

Arthur had been in a British Commando force which had raided a German headquarters in North Africa. He had been wounded and captured. The German officer in charge had chosen to ignore the standing order about shooting captured Commando men and had put Arthur in with a batch of other British prisoners who were being sent to Germany via Greece and Yugoslavia. In Yugoslavia, Arthur had escaped and spent the rest of the war fighting with the Tito Partisans. He had not troubled to return to England when the war ended, and had been one of the instructors provided by Tito to assist Markos.

In Arthur the Sergeant found a kindred spirit. They were both professional soldiers and had both served in *corps d'élite* as N.C.O.'s. Neither had any emotional ties with his native land. Both loved soldiering for its own sake. Above all, they shared the same outlook on matters of politics.

During his service with the Partisans, Arthur had listened to so much Marxist patter that he knew a great deal of it by heart. At moments of stress or boredom he would recite it at length and at lightning speed. It had disconcerted the Sergeant when he had heard it for the first time, and he had approached Arthur privately on the subject.

"I was not aware, Corporal," he had said in the clumsy mixture of Greek, English, and German they used in order to converse; "I did not think that you were a Red."

Arthur had grinned. "No? I'm one of the most politically reliable men in the outfit."

"So?"

"So. Don't I prove it? Look how many slogans I know. I can talk like the book."

"I see."

"Of course, I don't know what this dialectical-materialism stuff means, but then I could never understand what the Bible was all about either. At school we had to say bits of the Bible. I always used to get top marks for Scripture. Here I'm politically reliable."

"You do not believe in the cause for which we fight?"

"No more than you do, Sergeant. I leave that to the amateurs. Soldiering's my job. What do I want with causes?"

The Sergeant had nodded thoughtfully and glanced at the medal ribbons on Arthur's shirt. "Do you think, Corporal, that there is any possibility of our General's plans succeeding?" he had asked. Although they both held commissions in the Markos forces, they had chosen to ignore the fact in private. They had been N.C.O.'s in proper armies.

"Could be," Arthur said. "Depends on how many mistakes the other lot make, same as always. Why? What are you thinking about, Sarge? Promotion?"

The Sergeant had nodded. "Yes, promotion. If this revolution were to succeed, there might be big opportunities for men able to take them. I think that I, too, must take steps to become politically reliable."

The steps he had taken had proved effective, and his qualities as a natural leader had soon been recognized. By 1947 he was commanding a brigade, with Arthur as his second-in-command. When, in 1949, the Markos forces began to disintegrate, their brigade was one of the last to hold out in the Grammos area.

But they knew by then that the rebellion was over, and they were bitter. Neither of them had ever believed in the cause for which they had fought so long and hard and skillfully; but its betrayal by Tito and the Moscow Politburo had seemed an infamous thing.

" 'Put not your trust in princes,' " Arthur had quoted gloomily.

"Who said this?" the Sergeant had asked.

"The Bible. Only these aren't princes, they're politicians."

"It is the same." A faraway look had come into the Sergeant's eyes. "I think, Corporal, that in future we must trust only ourselves," he had said.

11

IT WAS just after dawn and the mountains above Florina were outlined against a pink glow in the sky when the old Renault deposited George and Miss Kolin outside the cinema where it had picked them up ten hours earlier. On George's instructions, Miss Kolin paid the driver and arranged with him to pick them up again that evening to make the same journey. They went to their hotel in silence.

When he got to his room, George destroyed the precautionary letter he had left there for the manager and sat down to draft a cable to Mr. Sistrom.

"CLAIMANT LOCATED IN STRANGE CIRCUMSTANCES," he wrote. "IDENTITY BEYOND REASONABLE DOUBT STOP COMPLEX SITUATION PREVENTS STRAIGHTFORWARD ACTION TO DELIVER HIM YOUR OFFICE STOP MAILING FULL EXPLANATION REPORT TODAY STOP MEANWHILE CABLE IMMEDIATELY TERMS OF EXTRADITION TREATY

IF ANY BETWEEN U.S. AND GREECE WITH SPECIAL REF-
ERENCE ARMED BANK ROBBERY. CAREY."

That, he thought grimly, should given Mr. Sistrom
something to gnaw on. He read it through again, strik-
ing out the unnecessary prepositions and conjunctions,
and then translated it into the code they had agreed on
for highly confidential messages. When he had finished
he looked at the time. The post office would not be
open for another hour. He would write to Mr. Sistrom
and mail the letter at the same time as he sent the
cable. He sighed. It had been an exhausting night—
exhausting in some unexpected ways. When the coffee
and buttered rolls he had ordered from the restaurant
arrived, he sat down to compose his report.

"In my last report," he began, "I told you of the
evidence I had been given by Madame Vassiotis and
of my consequent decision to return home as soon as
possible. Since then, as you will have gathered from
my cable, the picture has completely changed. I knew,
of course, that the inquiries instituted by Madame Vassiotis would reach the ears of all sorts of persons who,
for one reason or another, were regarded as criminals
by the authorities. I scarcely expected them to come to
the attention of the man we have been looking for.
Nevertheless, that is what happened. Twenty-four hours
ago I was approached by a man who stated that he had
friends who had information to give about Schirmer.
Subsequently Miss Kolin and I took a very uncomfortable trip to a secret destination somewhere in the mountains near the Yugoslav frontier. At the end of the
journey we were taken to a house and confronted by
a man who said he was Franz Schirmer. When I had
explained the purpose of our visit, I asked him various
pertinent questions, all of which he answered correctly.
I asked him then about the ambush at Vodena and his
subsequent movements. He told a fantastic story."

George hesitated; then he erased the word "fantastic"
—Mr. Sistrom would not like that sort of adjective—
and typed the word "curious" in its place.

And yet it *had* been fantastic, to sit there in the light
of the oil lamp listening to the great-great-grandson of

the hero of Preussisch-Eylau telling, in his broken English, the story of his adventures in Greece. He had spoken slowly, sometimes with a faint smile at the corners of his mouth, always with his watchful grey eyes on his visitors, reading and assessing them. The Dragoon of Ansbach, George thought, must have been very much the same kind of man. Where other men would succumb to physical disaster, men like these two Schirmers would always endure and survive. One had been wounded, had put his trust in God, had deserted, and lived to become a prosperous tradesman. The other had been left for dead, had put his trust in himself, had kept his wits about him, and lived to fight another day.

What the second Sergeant Schirmer had become, however, was a question that the Sergeant himself had made no attempt to answer.

His own account of himself had ended inconclusively at the time of the closing of the Yugoslav frontier by Tito, and with a bitter complaint against the manoeuvrings of the Communist politicians which had defeated the Markos forces. But George had very little doubt now about the nature of the Sergeant's subsequent activities. They had conformed to an ancient pattern. When defeated revolutionary armies disintegrated, those soldiers who feared for political reasons to go back home, or who had no homes to go back to, turned to brigandage. And since, quite clearly, neither the Sergeant nor Arthur was, to use Colonel Chrysantos's words, a "simple, deluded fanatic of the type that always gets caught," their gleanings in Salonika had almost certainly gone into their own pockets, and those of their men-at-arms. It was a delicate situation. Moreover, if he were not to seem suspiciously incurious, he would have to invite them somehow to explain their set-up in their own way.

It had been Arthur who had provided the opening.

"Didn't I tell you it'd be worth your while to come, Mr. Carey?" he said triumphantly when the Sergeant had finished.

"You did indeed, Arthur, and I'm very grateful. And of course I understand now the reason for all

he secrecy." He looked at the Sergeant. "I had no idea
hat fighting was still going on in this area."

"No?" The Sergeant drained his glass and set it
down with a bang. "It is the censorship," he said. "The
government hide the truth from the world."

Arthur nodded gravely. "Proper Fascist-imperialist
lackeys they are," he said.

"But we do not talk politics, eh?" The Sergeant
smiled as he filled Miss Kolin's glass. "It is not interesting for the beautiful lady."

She said something coldly in German and his smile
faded. For a moment he seemed to be reconsidering
Miss Kolin; then he turned to George cheerfully.

"Let us all fill our glasses and come to business,"
he said.

"Yes, let's do that," said George. He had given them
the reassuring impression that he was content with his
picture of them as simple revolutionaries still fighting
for a lost cause. That was enough. "I expect you'd like
to know a bit more about the whole affair, wouldn't
you, Sergeant?" he added.

"That is what I wish."

George told him the history of the case from the
beginning.

For a time the Sergeant listened politely, interrupting
only to ask for the explanation of a legal word or
phrase he did not understand. When Miss Kolin translated it into German he acknowledged the service each
time with nod. He seemed almost indifferent, as if he
were listening to something that was really no concern
of his. It was when George came to the part played in
the case by the account of the first Sergeant Schirmer's
exploits at Eylau that his attitude changed. Suddenly
he leaned forward across the table and began interrupting with abrupt, sharp-voiced questions.

"You say Franz Schirmer. He had the same name
and rank as me, this old man?"

"Yes. And he was roughly the same age as you were
when you dropped into Crete."

"So! Go on, please."

George went on, but not for long.

167

"Where was he wounded?"

"In the arm."

"As I was at Eben-Emael."

"No, he had a sabre cut."

"It does not matter. It is the same. Go on, please."

George went on again. The Sergeant's eyes were fixed on him intently. He interrupted again.

"Food? What food had he?"

"Some frozen potatoes he'd taken from a barn." George smiled. "You know, Sergeant, I've got the complete account of all this written out by Franz Schirmer's second son, Hans. That's the one who emigrated to America. He wrote it out for his children, to show them what a fine man their grandfather had been."

"You have this here?"

"I have a copy at the hotel in Florina."

"I may see it?" He was eager now.

"Sure. You can have it. You'll probably have the original eventually. I guess all the family papers are rightfully yours."

"Ah yes. The family papers." He nodded thoughtfully.

"But what Hans wrote isn't the whole story by any means. There were some things Franz Schirmer didn't tell his children."

"So? What things?"

George went on to tell him then about the meeting with Maria, about Mr. Moreton's investigation, and about his discovery of the truth in the army records at Potsdam.

The Sergeant listened without interruption now; and when George finished he remained silent for a moment or two staring down at the table in front of him. At last he looked up and there was a quiet smile of satisfaction on his face.

"That was a man," he said to Arthur.

"One of the boys, all right," Arthur agreed, nodding "same name and rank, too. Let's see—Dragoon were . . ."

But the Sergeant had turned to George again. "And this Maria. She was my great *Urgrossmutter?*"

"That's right. Her first son, Karl, was your *Urgross-vater*. But you see the strong case we have through knowing about the change of name. Amelia Schneider's first cousin was your grandfather, Friedrich, and he survived her. You remember him?"

The Sergeant nodded vaguely. "Yes. I remember."

"Legally, he inherited the money. You will inherit from him through your father. Of course your claim may have to be advanced through the German or maybe the Swiss courts. You may have to apply for Swiss papers first. I don't know. It depends on the attitude of the Pennsylvania court. Certainly we can expect the Commonwealth of Pennsylvania to fight. What the attitude of the Alien Property Custodian will be we don't yet know. It'll be tough, but I guess you won't mind that, eh?"

"No." But he did not appear either to understand or to be paying much attention to what George was saying. "I have never been to Ansbach," he said slowly.

"Well, you'll have plenty of time later on, I guess. Now, about the business side of it all. The law firm I represent are the attorneys for the administrator of the estate, so we couldn't act for you ourselves. You'd have to retain someone else. I don't know whether or not you can afford to put up money for the costs of fighting the case. They'd be pretty heavy. If you didn't want to do that we could recommend a good firm. They would act for you on a contingency basis. Explain it all, Miss Kolin, will you please?"

She explained. He listened absently and then nodded.

"You understand?" George asked.

"Yes. I understand. You do all."

"Very well. Now, how soon can you leave for America?"

George saw Arthur look at him sharply. Now the trouble was going to start.

The Sergeant frowned. "America?"

"Yes. We could travel together if you like."

"But I do not wish to go to America."

"Well, Sergeant, if you're going to claim your estate,

169

I'm afraid you'll have to go." George smiled. "The case can't be fought without you."

"You said that you would do all."

"I said we would recommend a firm of attorneys to represent you. But they can't fight the case without producing the claimant. They'll have to prove your identity and so on. The state and the Alien Property Custodian's lawyer will want to ask you a lot of questions."

"What questions?"

"Every sort of question. We'd better be quite clear about that. You're liable to have to account for every moment of your life, especially the bit since you were reported missing."

"That's torn it," said Arthur.

George misunderstood the remark with great care.

"Oh, I don't think the Sergeant has any cause to worry on that score," he said. "This is purely a domestic legal matter. The fact that he's been fighting in a civil war here is of no interest to Pennsylvania. We might run into some trouble getting a visa, but I think we could get over that in view of the special circumstances. Of course, the Greeks could make it tough for him if he wanted to return here afterwards, but beyond that there's nothing they can do. After all, it's not as if he'd committed some felony for which he could be extradited by the Greek government, is it?" He paused. "You'd better translate that, Miss Kolin," he added.

Miss Kolin translated. When she had finished, there was a tense silence. The Sergeant and Arthur stared at one another grimly. At last the Sergeant turned to George again.

"How much you say, this money?"

"Well, I'm going to be frank with you, Sergeant. Until I was quite sure who you were, I didn't want to make it sound too attractive. Now, you'd better know the facts. After various tax deductions, you stand to get about half a million dollars."

"Crikey!" said Arthur, and the Sergeant swore violently in German.

"Of course, that is only if you win the case. The Commonwealth is after the money too. Obviously they'll try to prove that you're an impostor and you'll have to be able to prove that you're not."

The Sergeant had risen impatiently and was pouring himself another glass of wine. George went on talking without a pause.

"It shouldn't be difficult, I think, if it's gone about in the right way. There are all sorts of possibilities. For instance, supposing for some reason you'd had your fingerprints taken—while you were in the German army, say—why then you wouldn't have any more to worry about. On the other hand . . ."

"Please!" The Sergeant held up his hand. "Please, Mr. Carey, I must think."

"Sure," said George. "I was being stupid. It must be quite a shock to realize that you're a rich man. It'll take time for you to get adjusted."

There was silence again. The Sergeant looked at Arthur and then they both looked at Miss Kolin sitting there impassively with her notebook. They could not say what was on their minds in front of her in Greek or German. Arthur shrugged. The Sergeant sighed and sat down by George again.

'Mr. Carey," he said, "I cannot so immediately decide what I must do. I must have time. There are so many things."

George nodded sagely as if he had suddenly understood the true nature of the Sergeant's dilemma. "Ah yes. I should have realized that, other difficulties apart, this situation presents you with quite a problem in revolutionary ethics."

"Please?"

Miss Kolin translated rapidly and with a faint sneer that did not please George in the least. But the Sergeant seemed not to notice it.

He nodded absently. "Yes, yes. That is so. I must have time to think about many things."

George thought that it was time for slightly plainer speaking. "There's one point I'd like to be clear about," he said. "That is, if you don't mind taking me into your confidence."

"Yes? A point?"

"Are you known to the Greek authorities under your own name?"

"Now, chum——" Arthur began warningly.

But George interrupted him. "Save it, Arthur. The Sergeant's going to have to tell me eventually anyway if I'm to be any use to him. You see that, don't you, Sergeant?"

The Sergeant thought for a moment, then nodded. "Yes. It is a good question, Corporal. I see his reason. Mr. Carey, I am known by another name to the police."

"Very well, then. I'm not interested in helping the Greek police. I'm concerned with the disposal of a big estate. Supposing that alias of yours could be kept out of the proceedings altogether—and I don't see why it shouldn't—would that make your decision easier?"

The Sergeant's shrewd eyes watched him steadily. "Would there be no photographs in the newspapers of such a lucky man, Mr. Carey?"

"Sure, there'd be pictures all over the front pages. Oh, I see. You mean that, names or no names, the fact that you'd been in Greece would be bound to attract attention here and the pictures would identify you anyway."

"So many persons know my face," said the Sergeant apologetically. "So you see, I must think."

"Yes, I see that," said George. He knew now that the Sergeant understood the position as clearly as he did. If the robbery or robberies in which he had been concerned were extraditable offenses, then any kind of publicity would be fatal to him. Among those who would know his face, for instance, would be the clerks in the Salonika branch of the Eurasian Credit Bank. The only thing the Sergeant did not understand was that George was aware of the true position. No doubt a day would come when it would be safe to enlighten him; in Mr. Sistrom's office perhaps. For the present, discretion was advisable.

"How long do you want to think, Sergeant?" he said.

"Until tomorrow. If you will tomorrow night come back we will speak again."

172

"O.K."

"And you will bring also my family papers?"

"I'll do that."

"Then *auf Wiedersehen*."

"*Auf Wiedersehen*."

"You will not forget the papers?"

"No, I won't forget, Sergeant."

Arthur took them back to the truck. He was silent on the way. It was evident that he, too, had plenty to think about. But when they were in the truck again and he was about to do up the canvas, he paused, and leaned on the tailboard.

"Do you like the Sarge?" he said.

"He's quite a guy, you must be very fond of him."

"Best pal in the world," said Arthur curtly. "I was just asking. I wouldn't like anything to happen to him, if you take my meaning."

George chuckled. "How would you like to be the most unpopular man in Philadelphia, Arthur?"

"Eh?"

"That's what I shall be if anything happens to Franz Schirmer."

"Oh-la-la! Sorry I spoke."

"Forget it. Say, what about taking it easy this time on some of those bends going down?"

"O.K., pal. You're the doctor. Easy it is."

The opening between the driver's seat and the rear of the truck had a flap over it, and during the drive down to the culvert George stuck a match so that Miss Kolin could examine the false number-plates again. She looked at them carefully and nodded. George extinguished the match impatiently. Any real hopes he might have had that the Sergeant would, after all, turn out to be only another simple-minded zealot of the Phengaros type had long since been abandoned. It was absurd to go on clutching at straws.

Promising to meet them again the following night at the same place, Arthur left them at the culvert. They stumbled back to the car, roused the old man from his sleep, and set out on the road back to Florina.

Although it was the first opportunity they had had

of talking privately since they had met the Sergeant, neither of them spoke for several minutes. Then it was Miss Kolin who at last broke the silence.

"What do you intend to do?" she asked.

"Cable the office for instructions."

"You will not inform the police?"

"Not unless the office tells me to. In any case, I'm by no means certain that we have anything more than vague suspicions to tell them."

"Is that your honest opinion?"

"Miss Kolin, I wasn't sent to Europe to act as a Greek police informer. I was sent to find the rightful claimant to the Schneider Johnson estate and produce him in Philadelphia. Well, that's what I'm doing. It's no concern of mine *what* he is here. He can be a brigand, a bandit, an outlaw, a traveling salesman, or the Metropolitan Archbishop of Salonika, for all I care. In Philadelphia, he's the rightful claimant to the Schneider Johnson estate, and what he is here doesn't affect his claim in the least."

"I should think it would considerably affect his value in court."

"That'll be his attorney's headache, not mine, and he can deal with it how he pleases. Anyway, why should you worry?"

"I thought that you believed in justice."

"I do. That's why Franz Schirmer is going to Philadelphia if I can get him there."

"Justice!" She laughed unpleasantly.

George was already tired; now he began to get annoyed.

"Look, Miss Kolin. You are engaged as an interpreter, not as a legal adviser or my professional conscience. Let's both stick to our jobs. At the moment, the only thing that matters is that, incredible as it may seem, this man is Franz Schirmer."

"He is also a German of the worst type," she said sullenly.

"I'm not interested in what type he is. All I'm concerned with is the fact that he exists."

There was silence for a moment and he thought that

the argument was ended. Then she began to laugh again.

"Quite a guy, the Sarge!" she said derisively.

"Now look, Miss Kolin," he began. "I've been very . . ."

But she was not listening any more. "The swine!" she exclaimed bitterly. "The filthy swine!"

George stared at her. She began pounding her knees with her fists and repeating the word "filthy."

"Miss Kolin. Don't you think . . ."

She rounded on him. "That girl in Salonika! You heard what he did?"

"I also heard what she did."

"Only for revenge after he had seduced her. And how many more has he treated that way?"

"Aren't you being a bit silly?"

She did not hear him. "How many more victims?" Her voice rose. "They are always the same, these beasts—killing, and torturing, and raping wherever they go. What do the Americans and British know of them? Your armies do not fight in your own lands. Ask the French about the Germans in their streets and in their houses. Ask the Poles and Russians, the Czechs, the Yugoslavs. These men are filthy slime on the land that suffers them. Filth! Beating and torturing, beating and torturing, bearing down with their strength, until they—until they—"

She broke off, staring blankly ahead as if she had forgotten what she had been going to say. Then, suddenly, she crumpled into a passionate storm of weeping.

George sat there as stolidly as his embarrassment and the lurching of the car would allow, trying to remember how many drinks he had seen her have since they had left Florina. It seemed to him that her glass had never once been empty while they had been at the Sergeant's headquarters, but he could not quite remember. Probably she had kept refilling it. If that were so, she must have had the best part of a bottle of plum brandy, as well as her after-dinner cognacs.

He had been too preoccupied to pay much attention to her.

She was sobbing quietly now. The old man driving had merely glanced around once and then taken no further interest. Presumably he was accustomed to distracted women. George was not. He was feeling sorry for her; but he was also remembering her pleasure in the anecdotes of Colonel Chrysantos, the man who knew "how to deal with Germans."

After a while, she went to sleep, her head cushioned in her arms against the back of the seat. The sky was beginning to lighten when she awoke. For a time she stared at the road, taking no notice of the wind blowing her hair about; then she took out a cigarette and tried to work her lighter. The breeze in the car was too strong for it and George, who was already smoking, passed his cigarette to her to light hers from. She thanked him quite normally. She made no reference to her outburst. No doubt she had forgotten about it. With Miss Kolin, he had decided now, anything was possible.

He finished his report to Mr. Sistrom and sealed it in an envelope. The post office might be open now he thought. He took the report and the cable and went downstairs.

He had left Miss Kolin over an hour before, when she had gone to her room. To his surprise, he saw her sitting in the café with the remains of a breakfast on the table in front of her. She had changed her clothes and was looking as if she had had a good night's sleep.

"I thought you were going to bed," he said.

"You said you were going to send a cable to your office. I was waiting to take it to the post office. They make so much chi-chi about cables there. They have so few. I did not think you would like to deal with them yourself."

"That's very good of you, Miss Kolin. Here it is. I've done my report, too. Air-mail that, will you?"

"Of course."

She left some money on the table for the breakfast and was going through the lobby to the street when the desk clerk came after her and said something in French. George caught the word *"téléphone."*

She nodded to the clerk and glanced at George—in an almost embarrassed way, he thought.

"My call to Paris," she said. "I had cabled my friends that I was on my way home. I wished to tell them that I would be delayed. How long do you think we will be?"

"Two or three days, I'd say." He turned to go. "Pretty good work that, to get through to Paris from here in an hour," he added.

"Yes."

He saw her enter the telephone booth and begin speaking as he went upstairs, back to his room to sleep.

At eight o'clock that evening they met the old man with the Renault again, and began their second journey to the Sergeant's headquarters.

George had slept fitfully for most of the day and felt a great deal wearier for having done so. In the faint hope that there might be a reply cable in from Mr. Sistrom, he had risen in the late afternoon and gone down to check. There had been nothing in. He had been disappointed but not surprised. Mr. Sistrom would have some thinking to do and some inquiries to make before he could send a useful reply. Miss Kolin had been out and, sitting beside her in the car, he noted that the leather satchel which she carried slung by a strap from her shoulder looked bulkier than usual. He decided that she had brought a bottle of brandy with which to fortify herself on the journey. He hoped, uneasily, that she would not hit it too hard.

Arthur was waiting for them at the same place and took the same precautions about shutting them in the truck. The night was even warmer than the previous one and George protested.

"Is all that still necessary?"

"Sorry, chum. Got to be done."

"It is a wise precaution," said Miss Kolin unexpectedly.

"Yes, that's right, miss." Arthur sounded as surprised as George felt. "Did you bring the Sarge's papers, Mr. Carey?"

"I did."

"Good. He's been worrying in case you'd forget. Can't wait to know about his namesake."

"I brought along a copy of an old photograph of him as well."

"You'll get a medal."

"What's been decided?"

"I don't know. We had a chat last night after you'd gone but—anyway, you talk to him about it. There we are! All tucked up now. I'll take it quiet."

They set off up the twisting, rock-strewn road to the ruined house and went through the same routine as before when they reached it. This time, however, as they stood waiting among the pine trees while Arthur warned the sentry of their approach, George and Miss Kolin had nothing to say to one another. Arthur returned and led them to the house.

The Sergeant greeted them in the hall, shaking hands with George and clicking heels to Miss Kolin. He smiled, but seemed secretly ill at ease as though doubtful of their goodwill. Miss Kolin, George was relieved to note, was her usual impassive self.

The Sergeant led them into the dining-room, poured out drinks, and eyed George's briefcase.

"You have brought the papers?"

"Sure." George opened the case.

"Ah!"

"And a photo of the Dragoon," George added.

"This is true?"

"It's all here." George took out a folder which he had brought from Philadelphia. Inside it there was a photostat or photograph of every important document in the case. "The Corporal didn't have time to read the interesting part when he searched my room." he added with a grin.

"Touché," said Arthur, unmoved.

The Sergeant sat down at the table, glass in hand, his eyes gleaming as if he were about to be served with some ambrosial meal. George began to lay the documents one by one in front of him, explaining as he did so the origin and importance of each. The Sergeant nodded understandingly at each explanation or turned to Miss Kolin for guidance; but George soon saw that there were only certain documents in which he was genuinely interested—those which directly concerned that first Franz Schirmer. Even a photograph of Martin Schneider, the soft-drinks potentate who had amassed the fortune which the Sergeant might inherit, produced no more than a polite exclamation. The photostats of Hans Schneider's Account, on the other hand, the church-register entries relating to the marriage of Franz, and the record of the baptism of Karl, he studied minutely, reading the German aloud to himself. The copy photograph of old Franz he handled as if it were a holy relic. For a long time he stared at it without speaking; then he turned to Arthur.

"You see, Corporal?" he said quietly. "Am I not like him?"

"Take away the beard and he's your spitting image," Arthur agreed.

And, indeed, for one who knew of the relationship, there was a strong resemblance between the two Schirmers. There was the same heavy strength in the two faces, the same determination in the two mouths, the same erectness; while the big hands grasping the arms of the chair in the daguerreotype and those grasping the photographic copy of it might, George thought, have belonged to the selfsame man.

There was a rap on the door and the sentry put his head in. He beckoned to Arthur.

Arthur sighed impatiently. "I'd better see what he wants," he said, and went out, shutting the door behind him.

The Sergeant took notice. He was smiling now over Hans Schneider's account of Eylau and the photostat of a page of the Dragoon's war diary, the one recording Franz Schirmer's desertion, which George had placed beside it. The old act of desertion seemed to give him special pleasure. From time to time he would glance at the old man's photograph again. George supposed that the Sergeant's own failure to return to Germany when an opportunity presented itself (he could have taken advantage of one of the amnesties) had been a kind of desertion. Perhaps, what the Sergeant was enjoying now was the reassuring intimation from the past that, contrary to the belief of his childhood, sinners were not obliged to dwell with devils always, and that outlaws and deserters, no less than fairy princes, might live happily ever after.

"Have you decided yet what you're going to do?" George asked.

The Sergeant looked up and nodded. "Yes. I think so, Mr. Carey. But first I would like to ask you some questions."

"I'll do my best . . ." he began.

But he never learned what the Sergeant's questions were. At that moment the door was flung open and Arthur came back into the room.

He slammed the door behind him, walked over to the table, and looked grimly at George and Miss Kolin. His face was pinched and grey with anger. Suddenly he threw two small, bright yellow tubes down on the table in front of them.

"All right," he said. "Which of you is it? Or is it both of you?"

The tubes were about an inch and a half long and half an inch thick. They looked as if they had been cut from bamboo and then coloured. The three round the table stared at them, then up at Arthur again.

"What is this?" snapped the Sergeant.

Arthur burst into an angry torrent of Greek. George glanced at Miss Kolin. Her face was still impassive, but she had gone very pale. Then Arthur stopped speaking and there was silence.

The Sergeant picked up one of the tubes, then looked from it to George and Miss Kolin. The muscles of his face set. He nodded to Arthur.

"Explain to Mr. Carey."

"As if he didn't know!" Arthur's lips tightened. "All right. Someone left a trail of these things from the culvert up here. One every fifty meters or so for someone else to follow. One of the lads coming up with a light spotted them."

The Sergeant said something in German.

Arthur nodded. "I put the rest out collecting them all before I came to report." He looked at George. "Any idea who might have dropped them, Mr. Carey? I found one of these two wedged between the canvas and the body of the truck, so don't start trying to play dumb."

"Dumb or not," George said steadily, "I don't know anything about them. What are they?"

The Sergeant got slowly to his feet. George could see a pulse going in his throat as he drew George's open briefcase towards him and looked inside. Then he shut it.

"Perhaps one should ask the lady," he said.

Miss Kolin sat absolutely rigid, looking straight in front of her.

Suddenly, he reached down and picked up her satchel from the floor by her chair.

"You permit?" he said, and thrusting his hand into it, drew out a tangle of thin cord.

He pulled on the cord slowly. A yellow tube came into view and then another, then a handful of the things, red and blue as well as yellow. They were strings of wooden beads of the kind used for making bead curtains. George knew now that it was not a bottle of brandy that had made the satchel so bulky. He began to feel sick.

"So!" The Sergeant dropped the beads on the table. "Did you know of this, Mr. Carey?"

"No."

"That's right, too," Arthur put in suddenly. "It was Little Miss Muffet here who wanted the canvas over the truck. Didn't want him to see what she was up to."

"For God's sake, Miss Kolin!" George said angrily. "What do you think you're playing at?"

She stood up resolutely, as if she were about to propose a vote of no-confidence at a public meeting, and turned to George. She did not even glance at Arthur or the Sergeant. "I should explain, Mr. Carey," she said coldly, "that, in the interests of justice and in view of your refusal to take any steps yourself in the matter, I considered it my duty to telephone Colonel Chrysantos in Salonika and inform him, on your behalf, that the men who robbed the Eurasian Credit Bank were here. On his instructions, I marked the route from the culvert, so that his troops could . . ."

The Sergeant's fist hit her full in the mouth and she crashed into the corner of the room where the empty bottles stood.

George leaped to his feet. As he did so the barrel of Arthur's gun jabbed painfully into his side.

"Stand still, chum, or you'll get hurt," Arthur said. "She's been asking for this and now she's going to get it."

Miss Kolin was on her knees, the blood trickling from her cut lip. They all stood watching her as she climbed slowly to her feet. Suddenly she picked up a bottle and flung it at the Sergeant. He did not move. It missed him by a few inches and smashed against the opposite wall. He stepped forward and hit her hard across the face with the back of his hand. She went down again. She had made no sound. She still made no sound. After a moment she began to get to her feet again.

"I'm stopping this," said George angrily, and started to move.

The gun dug into his side. "You try, chum, and you'll get a bullet in the kidneys. It's nothing to do with you, so shut up!"

Miss Kolin picked up another bottle. There was blood running from her nose now. She faced the Sergeant again.

"*Du Schuft!*" she said venomously, and hurled herself at him.

He brushed the bottle aside and hit her again in the face with his fist. When she fell this time she did not try to get up, but lay there gasping.

The Sergeant went to the door and opened it. The

182

sentry who had summoned Arthur was waiting there. The Sergeant beckoned him in, pointed to Miss Kolin, and gave an order in Greek. The sentry grinned and slung his rifle across his back. Then he went over to Miss Kolin and hauled her to her feet. She stood there swaying and wiping the blood from her face with her hand. He gripped her arm and said something to her. Without a word, and without looking at any of them, she began to walk towards the door.

"Miss Kolin—" George started forward.

She took no notice. The sentry pushed him aside and followed her out of the room. The door closed.

Sickened and trembling, George turned to face the Sergeant.

"Easy, chum," said Arthur. "None of the hero-to-the-rescue stuff. It won't wash here."

"Where's she being taken?" George demanded.

The Sergeant was licking the blood off one of his knuckles. He glanced at George, and then, sitting down at the table, took the passport from Miss Kolin's satchel.

"Maria Kolin," he remarked. "French."

"I asked where she's being taken."

Arthur was standing behind him still. "I wouldn't try getting tough, Mr. Carey," he advised. "Don't forget, you brought her here."

The Sergeant was examining the passport. "Born in Belgrade," he said. "Slav." He shut the passport with a snap. "And now we will talk a little."

George waited. The Sergeant's eyes rested on his.

"How did you find out, Mr. Carey?"

George hesitated.

"Talk fast, chum."

"The truck the Corporal brought us up in—it had slots for false number-plates and the plates were lying inside on the floor of the truck. They were the same numbers as those mentioned in the Salonika papers."

Arthur swore.

The Sergeant nodded curtly. "So! You knew this last night?"

"Yes."

"But *you* did not go to the police today?"

"What I did was to cable in code to my office to find out what the extradition treaty between America and Greece says about armed bank robbery."

"Please?"

Arthur explained in Greek.

The Sergeant nodded. "That was good. Did she know you do this?"

"Yes."

"Then why does she tell Chrysantos?"

"She doesn't like Germans."

"Ah, so?"

George looked down pointedly at the Sergeant's hands. "I understand her feelings."

"Easy, chum."

The Sergeant smiled enigmatically. "You understand her feelings? I do not think so."

The sentry came in, gave the Sergeant a key with a word of explanation; and went out again.

The Sergeant put the key in his pocket and poured himself a glass of plum brandy. "And now," he said, "we must think what is to be done. Your little friend is safely in a room upstairs. I think we must ask you also to stay, Mr. Carey. It is not that I do not trust you but that, at the moment, because you do not understand, you are feeling that you would like to destroy the Corporal and me. In two days, perhaps, when the Corporal and I have finished arranging our business, you may go."

"Do you intend to keep me here by force?"

"Only if you are not wise and do not wish to stay."

"Aren't you forgetting why I came here?"

"No. I will give you my decision in two days, Mr. Carey. Until then, you stay."

"Supposing I told you that unless Miss Kolin and I are released immediately you'll have as much chance of inheriting that estate as that sentry outside."

"Your office in America will be very sad. Arthur explained to me."

George felt himself reddening. "Does it occur to you that, trail or no trail, Colonel Chrysantos won't take

184

very long to find this place now? In two or three hours he may have you surrounded by Greek troops."

Arthur laughed. The Sergeant smiled grimly.

"If that is so, Mr. Carey, Chrysantos will be in trouble with his government. But you need not worry. If this bad Colonel comes, we will protect you. A glass of wine? No? Brandy? No? Then, since you are tired, the Corporal will show you where you can sleep. Good night." He nodded dismissal and began to go through the photostats again, putting those that interested him specially into a separate pile.

"This way, chum."

"Just a moment. What about Miss Kolin, Sergeant?"

The Sergeant did not look up. "You do not have to worry about her, Mr. Carey. Good night."

Arthur led the way; George followed him; the sentry brought up the rear. They went upstairs to a derelict room with a straw mattress on the floorboards. There was also a bucket. The sentry brought in an oil lamp.

"It's only for a couple of nights, Mr. Carey," said Arthur—the hotel receptionist apologizing to a valued client who has arrived unexpectedly. "You'll find the palliasse fairly clean. The Sarge is very keen on hygiene."

"Where's Miss Kolin?"

"Next room." He perked his thumb. "But don't you worry about her. It's a better room than this."

"What did the Sergeant mean about Chrysantos getting into trouble with the government?"

"If he tried to surround us? Well, the Greek frontier's nearly a kilometre away. We're on Yugoslav territory. I'd have thought you'd have guessed."

George digested this disconcerting news while Arthur adjusted the lamp wick.

"What about the frontier patrols?"

Arthur hung the lamp on a hook jutting out from the wall. "You want to know too much, chum." He went to the door. "No lock on this door, but, just in case you're thinking of sleep-walking, there's a wide-awake sentry here on the landing, and he's trigger-happy. Get the idea?"

185

"I get it."

"I'll give you a call when it's time for breakfast. Pleasant dreams."

About an hour had gone by when George heard the Sergeant come upstairs and say something to the sentry.

The sentry replied briefly. A moment or two later George heard the sound of a key being inserted in the door of the next room—the room Arthur had said was Miss Kolin's.

With some idea of protecting her, George got up quickly from the mattress on which he had been lying and went to the door. He did not open it immediately. He heard Miss Kolin's voice and the Sergeant's. There was a pause, then the sound of the door being shut. The key turned in the lock once more.

For a while, he thought the Sergeant had gone, and went back to the corner where his mattress was. Then he heard the Sergeant's voice again, and hers. They were talking in German. He went to the wall and listened. The tone of their voices was curiously conversational. He was aware of a strange uneasiness and his heart began to beat too fast.

The voices had ceased now, but soon they began once more, and softly, as if the speakers did not wish to be overheard. Then there was silence for a long time. He lay down again on the mattress. Minutes went by; then, in the silence, he heard her utter a fierce, shuddering cry of passion.

He did not move. After a while there were low voices again. Then nothing. He became aware for the first time of the sound of the cicadas in the night outside. He was at last beginning to understand Miss Kolin.

12

GEORGE WAS kept for two days and three nights at the Sergeant's headquarters.

On the first day, the Sergeant left the house soon after dawn, and returned when it was dark. George spent the day in the room downstairs, and had his meals there with Arthur. He did not see either the Sergeant or Miss Kolin. After that first night, she was moved to another room in an annex to the house and food was taken to her by one of the sentries. When George asked if he could see her, Arthur shook his head.

"Sorry, chum. No can do."

"What's happened to her?"

"I'll give you three guesses."

"I want to see her."

Arthur shrugged. "I don't mind whether you see her or not. It's just that *she* doesn't want to see *you*."

"Why not?"

"The Sarge is the only one she wants to see."

"Is she all right?"

"Fit as a fiddle." He grinned. "Cut lip, of course, and a bruise or two, but radiant as a bride. You wouldn't know her."

"How much longer is this going on?"

"Search me. I'd say it had only just started."

"After what happened, it doesn't make sense."

Arthur looked at him with some amusement. "I expect you've been nicely brought up. I told you she'd been asking for it, didn't I? Well, she got it, and very nice too. I've never seen the Sarge take such a fancy to a girl before."

"A fancy!" George was getting angry.

"I wouldn't mind betting she was a virgin," Arthur mused; "or as good as."

"Oh, for God's sake!"

"What's the matter, chum? Sour grapes?"

"I don't think there's much point in discussing it. Did Colonel Chrysantos turn up?"

"The sheriff's posse, you mean? Sure. They're sitting on their backsides, like twerps, just on the other side of the frontier. Waiting for something to happen."

"Or maybe waiting for Miss Kolin and me to turn up. Supposing the American Legation's brought into this and they start complaining to Belgrade. Going to be a bit awkward for you, isn't it?"

"You'll be back before they finish even *talking* about doing anything. And when you do get back, you'll begin to think again about all the fuss your office is going to make over the Sarge, and say it was all a mistake."

"Got it all worked out, haven't you? I don't see what you had to get so upset about."

"No? For one thing they've arrested that poor old sod who drove you. That's not so funny, is it?"

"How do you know?"

"We had word from Florina this morning."

"How?"

"Ask no questions, you'll be hold no lies. I'll tell you this, though. The *comitadjis* have been using these hills for fifty years or more. There's not much you can't get away with in these parts if you know the ropes. Don't forget that they're Macedonians on both sides of the frontier. When it comes to small-scale work like this, the Chrysantos boys haven't got an earthly."

"What'll happen to the driver?"

"That depends. He's an old *comitadji,* so he won't say where he got his orders from, no matter what they do to him. But it's awkward. He isn't the only one in Florina. There's old Ma Vassiotis, for instance. They might have a go at her. You know, if the Sarge hadn't changed things round a bit, I'd be inclined to go

188

up and give your Miss What's-her-name another bashing myself."

"Supposing I were to tell Chrysantos that I hired the car and told the old man where to go."

"He might believe you. But how did *you* know where to go?"

"I'd say you told me."

Arthur laughed. "Proper lawyer, aren't you?"

"Would it matter to you?"

"Not a tuppenny damn."

"O.K., then."

Arthur was cleaning a pistol. George watched him for a while in silence. At last he said: "Supposing there had been no question of the Sergeant's going to America. Would you have gone on with this racket of yours?"

Arthur looked up, then shook his head. "No. I reckon we've just about had it now."

"Having pulled off the big job?"

"Maybe. Time to move on anyway." He bent over the pistol again.

"Got plenty of dough put away?" George said after a moment or two.

Arthur looked up, startled. "I've never met anyone with such terrible manners," he said.

"Come off it, Arthur."

But Arthur was genuinely shocked. "How would you like it if I was to ask you how much money you had in the bank?" he said indignantly.

"All right. Tell me something else, then. How did it start? The Sergeant kept very quiet about that. What happened in the end to that Markos brigade you both commanded?"

Arthur shook his head sadly. "Always asking questions. I suppose it's being a lawyer."

"I have an inquiring mind."

"Just plain nosy-parkering, my mother would have called it."

"You forget that, at present, I'm the Sergeant's legal adviser. Between a man and his legal adviser there should be no secrets."

Arthur uttered an obscene four-letter word and went back to his cleaning.

But the following evening he came back to the subject of his own accord. George had still seen nothing of either the Sergeant or Miss Kolin and a suspicion had been forming in his mind. He began to ask questions again.

"What time's the Sergeant coming back today?"

"Don't know, chum. When we see him, I expect." Arthur was reading a Belgrade newspaper that had arrived mysteriously during the day. Now he threw it down in disgust. "Lot of nonsense in that paper," he said. "Ever read *The News of the World?* London paper that is."

"No, I've never seen it. Is the Sergeant in Greece or Albania today?"

"Albania?" Arthur laughed, but, as George opened his mouth to ask another question, he went on. "You were asking what happened to us when we packed up fighting. We were up near the Albanian frontier then."

"Oh, yes?"

Arthur nodded reminiscently. "You ought to have a look at Mount Grammos if you ever get the chance," he said. "Wonderful scenery up that way."

The Grammos massif had been one of the first strongholds of the Markos forces; it came to be one of the last.

For weeks the brigade's position in the area had been deteriorating steadily. The trickle of deserters had become a stream. There came a day in October when important decisions had to be taken.

The Sergeant had been on his feet for fourteen hours or more, and his hip was paining him, when at last he gave orders to bivouac for the night. Later, the officer in charge of an outlying picket caught two deserters from another battalion and sent them to brigade headquarters to be dealt with.

The Sergeant looked at the men thoughtfully and then gave orders for them to be executed. When they had been led away, he poured himself a glass of wine and nodded to Arthur to do the same. They drank their wine in silence, Then, the Sergeant refilled the glasses.

"Does it occur to you, Corporal," he said, "that those two men may have been setting their brigade commander and his second-in-command a good example?"

Arthur nodded. "It's been occurring to me for days, Sarge. We haven't a hope in hell."

"No. The best we can hope for is that they will starve us to death."

"They're beginning to do that already."

"I have no wish to be a martyr of the revolution."

"Neither have I. We've done our jobs, Sarge, as well as we knew how and a bit over. *And* we've kept faith. That's more than those bastards at the top can say."

" 'Put not your trust in princes.' I have remembered that, you see. I think the time has come to seek our independence."

"When do we go?"

"Tomorrow night would not be too soon."

"When they find out us two have gone, you won't see the rest of them for dust. I wonder how many'll get through."

"The ones who always get through, the *comitadji* types. They will hide away in their hills as they have done before. They will be there when we want them."

Arthur was startled. "When we want them? I thought you said something about independence."

The Sergeant filled his glass again before he replied. "I have been thinking, Corporal," he said at last, "and I have a plan. The politicians have used us. Now we will use them."

He stood up and limped over to his kit bag for the tin box in which he kept his cigars.

Arthur watched him with something that he knew was very like love. He had a profound respect for his friend's planning ability. Surprising things sometimes emerged from that hard, heavy head.

"How use them?" he said.

"The idea came to me several weeks ago," said the Sergeant. "I was thinking of that history of the Party which we were once compelled to read. You remember?"

"Sure. I read mine without cutting the pages open."

The Sergeant smiled grimly. "You missed some important things, Corporal. I will give you my copy to read." He lighted a cigar luxuriously. "I think that it is quite possible that from being mere soldiers we may soon become soldiers of fortune."

"It was dead easy," Arthur said. "The Sarge had got hold of a list of all the secret Party members and sympathizers in the Salonika area, and we sorted out those that worked in banks and in the offices of businesses with big payrolls. Then we approached them and gave them their big chance to serve the Party in its hour of need, just as the book said the old Bolshies had done. We could always say we'd denounce them if they got suspicious, but we haven't had any trouble of that kind. I tell you, every single job we've done, we've had a man or woman on the inside, helping us for the honour and glory of the Party." He laughed contemptuously. "Flies in the Ointment, Unite! They couldn't wait to ditch the people they were working for. Some of them would torture their own mothers if the Party wanted them to, and be glad to do it. 'Yes, Comrade. Certainly, Comrade. Glad to be of service, Comrade!' It's made me sick sometimes to hear them," he added self-righteously.

"Still, you did pretty well out of it, didn't you?"

"Maybe we did, but I still don't like people who bite the hand that feeds them."

"Surely, it must have taken quite a bit of courage for some of these people to act on their convictions to the extent of helping you."

"I'm not so sure," said Arthur sourly. "If you ask me, these political convictions that make it O.K. to play someone else a dirty trick behind their backs have something pretty phony about them."

"You're quite a moralist, Arthur. What about the trick *you* were playing?"

"I'm not pretending to be better than I am. It's these phonies I can't stand. You should talk to some of them. Clever. Know all the answers. Prove anything you like. The sort you *don't* want with you if you're going out on a patrol, because, if things get sticky, *they're* the ones who'll start looking round for a reason for everybody to chuck in their hands and go home."

"Does the Sergeant feel the same way about these things?"

"Him?" Arthur laughed. "No. He doesn't bother. You see, *I* think there are all kinds of people. He doesn't. He thinks there are only two kinds—those you'd want with you when things are bad, and those you wouldn't have at any price." He smiled slyly and added: "And he makes up his mind real quick."

George lit his last cigarette and stared thoughtfully at Arthur for a moment. The suspicion suddenly became a certainty. He screwed up the empty pack and tossed it on the table.

"Where are they, Arthur?" he said.

"Where are who?" Arthur's face was all innocence.

"Come on, Arthur! Let's stop playing games. They were here last night, I know, because I heard the Sergeant come in around midnight and start talking to you. But this morning neither he nor Miss Kolin was here. At least, I didn't see him, and no food's been taken up to her. So where are they?"

"I don't know."

"Think again."

"I don't know, Mr. Carey, and that's a fact."

"Has he gone for good?"

Arthur hesitated and then shrugged. "Yes, he has."

George nodded. He had suspected, but, now that he knew for certain, the news came as a blow. "What am I being kept here for?" he asked.

"He's got to have time to get clear."

"Clear of me?"

"No, clear of this country." Arthur leaned forward earnestly. "You see, supposing you went back and Chrysantos started on you, and you blew the gaff about his being on the way out. I don't say you'd mean to, but he's a cunning bastard, that one. You can see it might be awkward.

"Yes, I see. He'd already decided what he was going to do. I think he might have told me."

"He asked me to, Mr. Carey. I was going to wait until after supper, just to be on the safe side, but you may as well know now. You see, there wasn't much time. We've been all fixed up to go for days. He made the final arrangements yesterday and just came back to ask her if she wanted to go too."

"And she did?"

"Like a shot. Can't keep her hands off him. Proper case it is."

"Isn't he afraid she'll try and turn him in again?"

Arthur laughed. "Don't be silly, chum. She's been waiting for a man like that all her life."

"I still don't get it."

"I expect you're like me," Arthur said consolingly. "I like it a little more on the quiet side myself. But about the money—"

"Yes, about the money."

"We talked it over, him and me, Mr. Carey, and we came to a conclusion. He couldn't have claimed it. You see that, don't you? You talked about extradition and all that, but that's not the point. Extradition or not, everything would have had to come out. That'd be no good. He's going to start a new life under a new name, with all this behind him. He hasn't got half a million dollars or anything like, but he's got enough to go on with. If he claimed that money he'd be a marked man. You know that as well as I do."

"He could have told me this the first time."

"He only wanted his family papers, Mr. Carey. You can't blame him for that."

"And he just had me stringing along so that I wouldn't make trouble. I get it." George sighed. "All right. What's his new name going to be? Schneider?"

"Now, you don't want to be bitter, chum. He liked you and he's very grateful."

After a moment or two George looked up. "What about you?"

"Me? Oh, I'll be getting along, too, by and by. It's easier for me, being British. There are all sorts of places I can go. I might even join the Sarge if I feel like it."

"Then, you *do* know where he's going?"

"Yes, but I don't know *how* he's going. He might be on a ship in Salonika at this very moment for all I know. But I couldn't say for certain. What I don't know, nobody can make me tell."

"So you're just here to look after me. Is that it?"

"Well, I've got to pay off the boys, too, and clear up generally. I'm the adjutant, you might say."

There was a silence. He looked round the room moodily. His eyes met George's. Unsuccessfully, for once, he tried to grin.

"I tell you what, chum," he said. "Now that the Sarge's gone and everything, I reckon we're both a bit down in the mouth today. We got hold of some German wine once. Kept it for special occasions, like last night. What about you and me having a bottle between us now?"

The sun was shining when George awoke the following morning. He looked at his watch and saw that it was eight o'clock. On the two previous mornings, Arthur had roused him, with a good deal of military noise, at seven.

He listened. The house was quite silent and the cicadas outside seemed very loud. He went and opened the door of his room.

There was no sentry on duty there. The "boys" had evidently been paid off. He went downstairs.

In the room where they had eaten their meals, Arthur had left a note and a letter for him.

George looked at the note first.

Well chum [it said], *I hope you have not got too much of a hangover. There's a letter here that Sergeant Schirmer left for you before he went. Sorry I can't lend you my razor today as it's the only one I've got. When you want to go back to dear old Civilization just walk*

*up through the trees past the place we parked the truck
and then take the right fork. You can't miss it. It's less
than a mile away. Nobody on this side will interfere
with you. You will soon meet a patrol on the other
side. Don't forget to do your best for that old driver.
It's been nice knowing you. All the best. Arthur.*

The letter from the Sergeant was in Miss Kolin's
angular handwriting.

DEAR MR. CAREY [he read],
*I have asked Maria to write this for me so that
the meaning of what I feel and have to say will be
clear and properly expressed in your language.*

*First, allow me to apologize for having left you so
suddenly and discourteously, without taking my
leave of you. No doubt, by the time you read this,
the Corporal will have explained to you the situation
and also the reasons for my decision not to attempt to
go with you to America. I trust that you will understand. I was naturally disappointed, as I have always
wished to see something of your country. Perhaps
some day it will be possible.*

*And now, permit me to express my gratitude to
you and to those of your office who sent you. Maria
has told me of your persistence and determination to
find a man you had so much reason to believe dead.
It is a good thing to be able to go on a little further
when those with less spirit are ready to turn back. I
am sorry that you will have no more valuable a
reward than my gratitude. Yet that I offer you
sincerely, my friend. I would have been glad to
receive so much money if it had been possible, but
not more glad than I am now to possess the documents you brought me.*

*The money I cannot think of with great emotion.
It is a large sum, but I do not think it has to do with
me. It was earned in America by an American. I
think it is just that, if there is no other heir but me,
the American State of Pennsylvania should have it.
My true inheritance is the knowledge you have*

196

brought me of my blood and of myself. So much has changed and Eylau is long ago, but hand clasps hand across the years and we are one. A man's immortality is in his children. I hope I shall have many. Perhaps Maria will bear them. She says that she will wish to.

The Corporal tells me that you will be so kind as to speak discreetly for the driver who was arrested. Maria asks that, if possible, you will give him her typewriter and the other things she left in Florina so that he may sell them and have the money. His name is Douchko. She sends you also her apologies and her thanks. So now, my friend, there is only left for me to thank you again and to wish you happiness in your life. I hope we may meet again.

Yours very sincerely,
FRANZ SCHIRMER

The signature was in his own writing, very neat and clear.

George put the letters in his pocket, got his briefcase from his room, and walked up through the pine trees. It was a fine, fresh morning and the air was good. He began to think out what he would have to say to Colonel Chrysantos. The Colonel was not going to be pleased; neither was Mr. Sistrom. The whole situation, in fact, was most unfortunate.

George wondered why it was, then, that he kept laughing to himself as he walked on towards the frontier.

ABOUT THE AUTHOR

ERIC AMBLER was born in London in 1909. Following his graduation from London University, he served an apprenticeship in engineering, toured England as a vaudeville comedian, and wrote songs and advertising copy. From 1937 to 1940, Mr. Ambler wrote four of his most successful novels: *Background to Danger, Cause for Alarm, A Coffin for Dimitrios* and *Journey into Fear*. In the British Army from 1940 to 1946 he was in charge of all military training, morale and education films. After the war Mr. Ambler wrote and produced a number of motion pictures for the J. Arthur Rank organization. His screenplay for Nicholas Monsarrat's *The Cruel Sea* was nominated for an Academy Award. In 1951, *Judgment on Deltchev,* his first novel in eleven years, was published. This was followed by *The Schirmer Inheritance, State of Siege, Passage of Arms, The Light of Day* and *A Kind of Anger*. Mr. Ambler's anthology of spy stories, *To Catch a Spy,* was recently published. He lives in Bel Air, California.

These books?
Fiction.
Keep telling
yourself that
as you read.